A Child of Magic

By Christine Olivia Dargas

Cover and Illustration by Mike Dargas

First published 2018

ISBN 978-1-970124-00-2

Colophon

Text by Christine Olivia Dargas

Cover and illustration by Mike Dargas

Designed by Marin Joe Garcia using Adobe® InDesign.®

The typefaces used are Berthold Baskerville for the body
text and chapter titles. Designed by Hermann Berthold,
Based on John Baskerville's types first issued between 1752
and 1757 in Birmingham, England, H. Berthold released its
version in 1961. Baskerville types are known for their clarity
and legibility. Berthold's version is a highly readable design,
making it a popular choice for books and other longer texts.

Contents

To the inner child. The one that sees with eyes of wonder and heart aglow.

Chapter I

Loving Mother Earth

One morning, Lana was on the swing set imagining she was a bird rising high into the sky. Like a mighty eagle, she soared gracefully through the clouds to touch the sun with her glittering wings. Expressing herself freely in fluid movement and fearless measure, Lana was thoroughly enjoying herself when she heard a familiar song. It was beckoning from the direction of the trees, and she was a good listener. She walked past the edge of the playground towards the music and lush greenery.

Lana frolicked through the opening of the woods as it morphed into an enchanted forest, alive with multicolored trees and flowers that fluttered to the music. Vivid butterflies and birds flew, chirping along with the sweet melody, and beautiful creatures like the fox and the deer were playful. Presence was felt through the spirit of a willow tree, singing to Lana, inviting her to reconnect with nature.

Lana Livia was a child of magic, miraculous and

extraordinary as ever a young spirit was, a being made of love and light, a sensitive soul closely connected to her truth. She loved being out in the open, near trees, or the ocean breeze. When in nature, she felt loved and supported through her connection to Mother Earth, and when detached, her dazzling imagination helped her cope with a big world that didn't believe in magic.

A couple of dainty, rosy fairies flew above Lana's head as she danced towards the singing tree. They gifted her with a daisy-flower crown, wholly welcoming her to the forest. They sang in her ear,

"We are loved, we are related in the light.
You are loved, you are the light.
Swing this way, let us remind you of your ways.
Sweet as the sun, Magic child we are one."

Bright-eyed with amazed delight, she giggled and twirled around.

"Thank you." Lana overflowed with so much joy and gratitude that the entire forest felt it and was kindled with pleasure.

The fairies kissed her cheeks lightly and then guided her to the tree that sang.

"I adore you dear one," the willow tree laughed with adoration as her branches stirred and the leaves gently wove around Lana affectionately. "You have a wondrous imagination, and I delight in your connection to your truth and magic."

"Wow. Thank you. All of this is very beautiful, but who are you?" asked Lana.

"You know who I am; you simply forget. I am Mother Earth, Pachamama, Mama Gaia, whatever you would like to call me in this moment, child. I am part of you, this forest, and always here, whether you see me or not."

Lana faintly remembered her. She resonated with the words Pachamama and appreciated the whimsical way it made her feel when she said the name aloud.

"It is a truth that will soon be forgotten through your human experience. You are only thinking about it now because at this moment you are in the stages of forgetting. That is normal, but what is unique about you is that your imagination is unyielding. You are a powerful force with your light and will come back to me in due time."

Lana beamed with this golden aura that expanded out into the forest as she hugged the willow's bark tightly.

"Pachamama, I will try to remember this forever. I wish to hold onto my truth and be the light in the world for others."

"You are a child of magic. One day you will forget and then remember who you truly are. Thus you will shine with brilliant light, reminding others of their inner radiance," said Pachamama. "All in right timing."

Like a nursery rhyme sung by a mother to her infant, Pachamama began to sing in a way that was otherworldly. It was language beyond words but understood as a feeling of deep love. Lana looked around at all the beauty around her. Although she didn't remember it, Lana had had many special moments here and loved it. She didn't recollect the details, but she felt a familiar comfort.

Lana climbed the willow to find the home of her beloved green-and-red glowing fairy sisters Juniper and Marigold. She loved their beds made of blue moss, the pillows of mushroom heads, and how intricate the tiny yellow flowers were that decorated their living area. It was wondrous, and Lana had spent many nights trying to recreate it with her toy set at home. She sat with a broad smile on her face, as the fairies brought over tiny translucent flowers filled with sweet nectar to sip on. Always such a delicious treat.

"I've had this before, haven't I? I remember this taste. It's delicious," said Lana, relishing the sweet flowery flavors.

"It's your favorite," said Juniper as she sparkled with emerald-colored glee. "We've missed you a lot. All of us have. The fox was whining over you last night, and so were we. So this is so wonderful to see you here. How are you in this moment?"

"I'm wonderful. I was just flying with my imagination, and now I'm here, and I'm just so happy to really be here," Lana said honestly. She paused and then remembered how throughout her life she had been here many times before. She was so glad to have this memory back even if it would fade away again. A few creatures including the fox gathered below her and called softly. They wanted to play too. The fox was thrilled and couldn't wait to snuggle, and so he jumped and climbed up the tree. Lana hugged him close to her and caressed his soft fur.

"Lana, I've missed you!" cried Felix the fox.

"Hi Felix. Oh, I've missed you too. It seems I'm beginning to forget our visits. It makes me sad to admit that I can't remember the last time I saw you, but I do remember you of course. I know that must be confusing. I'm sorry," said Lana and she hugged him tighter.

"That's okay Lana. We all knew that would happen. That's why we decided to make you something special, so you could remember us, or at least have a part of us always with you," said Felix as he uncovered the most extraordinary necklace ever seen.

The necklace was made from sage-green shrubbery and little red flowers strung together to hold beautiful orange carnelian and rose-quartz stones. In the center, it had a tiny glass jar filled with stardust from the fairies. It was floral, sturdy, and charmed to withstand the tides of time.

The willow's branches gently grazed around Lana

affectionately.

"The necklace will remind you when the time is right. For now, enjoy this moment with your friends from the forest," said Pachamama.

Juniper and Marigold carefully took it from Lana's hands and placed it around her neck. Lana was overcome with appreciation. She could barely contain all the love that was felt in her heart and soul.

"I'll never take it off, it's incredible. Thank you," said Lana as tears of gratefulness formed in the corner of her eyes.

The fox, the fairies, and Lana hugged and giggled with joy and continued to play in the tree. Lana felt like a mythical princess, adored and beloved by the forest. Such abundant love was nourished in nature.

Lana was a unique child, born into this world by a young mother and father who separated shortly after her birth. Ray had unfortunately left when Lana was almost two. Thus, Lana was raised by her mother Rachel and by her grandmother, whom she called Nana. Like all families, they did their very best.

Most mornings, when Nana was working, Lana and Rachel could be found at a small playground near their tiny yellow home in an ordinary suburb near the California coast. When the weather was pleasant, it was fitting for Rachel to do her work on the park benches, and for Lana to express her energy with play. This was no ordinary playground of course, but was next to the lush forest where Lana could connect with nature and be free with her self-expression.

Lana was well known for wandering into the woods whenever she could sneak away. Rachel couldn't be bothered to search for her daughter. Instead, she grew impatient and yelled, "Lana get over here where I can see you! I'm trying to get this work done!"

Lana was startled, and her eyes filled with tears. Yelling always had that impact on her. She scrambled down the tree and back to the concrete playground. She stumbled, her crown crumbled, and all the creatures ran off, the enchantment fading. The necklace was intact, but her feelings were deeply hurt, and she sobbed.

"I'm sorry I yelled at you, baby. I just don't want you wandering off like that," Rachel said remorsefully. She cradled Lana in her lap, uncovering a piece of chocolate from her bag. Chocolate always soothed Lana.

"Where did you get that necklace, baby?"

"from the forest" said Lana.

"It's stunning. Did Nana give it to you?"

"I got it from my best friends," Lana said firmly and ate more chocolate.

Silence fell over them as Rachel thought to herself that Lana didn't have any friends yet. She assumed Nana must have surprised her with it.

Lana was absorbed by the chocolate, but she felt

the forest of enchantment still living and singing.

She wished she could bring the essence of nature out into the world. She vowed to herself that she'd embody the ways of the forest as best she could and use her imagination to alchemize the world around her. She placed her left hand on the necklace and set the intention with her heart and soul.

A lovely orange-spotted squirrel ran past Pacham-ama, back into the deep woods eager to share the tale of Lana's visit and the marvelous necklace. Each step he took lit up his path with blue and purple moss that glowed vibrantly. The forest was living and breath-ing with enchantment; you needed only be open to notice it.

Chapter II

Wings

Lana's yellow house was a quaint and cute one-story home, with three small bedrooms and a tiny mostly dirt yard with a single sycamore tree in the backyard. To Lana, the yard was expansive, and she imagined it as the desert with the tree as an oasis. She'd pretend to struggle to survive the harsh sandstorms and the heat until she reached what wasn't a mirage, but a haven of a tree with its shade and flowing leaves for her to rest beneath.

Lana was not only a very imaginative five-year-old but a curious one who loved books. She found reading to be intriguing and quite exciting. She liked climbing the backyard sycamore as high as she could to read her favorite stories. The tree was beloved and appreciated for the way it supported her.

Nana was a cleaning lady for a wealthy family in a nearby neighborhood. It was a daily job and easy for Nana to work hard and quickly so she could get home to Lana just in time for Rachel to get to work or run errands on the weekends.

On this particular weekend, Rachel was making banana pancakes. She liked to make pancakes on the weekends to break their daily cereal routine before heading out. Lana was thinking of her dreams while she walked into the kitchen for breakfast.

"Good morning baby, how did you sleep? Did you dream?"

"Very good Mama, I remembered how to fly last night."

"That's nice. Honey, are you ever going to take off that necklace?"

"No, I'm not. Please stop asking," said Lana plainly.

"Well okay, fine. So, you mean you dreamt you could fly?" said Rachel with a slight edge to her voice.

"No, I dreamed so I could remember how to fly! I remembered that I had golden feathered wings that were larger than my body. They were connected to my shoulders, and all I needed to do was want to fly and then I could. My wings were glittering, and when I flew, they shimmered like the rainbow in the sun. It was so beautiful." Lana sighed. "But when I woke up I was sad they were gone. It's sad that we forgot how to fly."

"Oh baby, that's a lovely dream, but I'm pretty sure we never had wings to begin with," Rachel said dismissively as she flipped a pancake onto Lana's plate.

"We did Mama, we just forgot how to use them,

just like we forget how to use a lot of things."

"Okay, baby. Eat your pancakes, they're getting cold."

Lana didn't mention the fact that after this dream, she woke to find an angel in the hallway. Her eyes were sleepy from just rising, but she saw its glowing aura and felt its presence, and with a blink, it vanished. She smiled and thought about it while she munched on her pancakes. She'd keep that moment to herself. Her mother might not appreciate it anyway.

Rachel was the opposite of imaginative. An accountant at a big-chain clothing company called Soriety, she typically seemed a bit distant and distracted, as her attention was often on work. Her priority was to provide a life she was proud of for herself and her daughter. Being this way closed her off to the wonders in which her daughter was living in.

Rachel was raised by sweet Nana and a sometimes-harsh father. Her father had been a marine in the Vietnam War and he had died before Lana had been born. Growing up, he hadn't shown Rachel much affection, but he had instilled in her a serious discipline that she carried with her. She had wanted to make him proud, so Rachel had always been an obedient child. That is, until she had met Lana's father during her last year of high school. This was how she rebelled against her father. Ray was the new kid in school and Rachel couldn't resist his free-spirited and charming demeanor. They became high-school sweethearts, and Lana came into this world, a lovely rebel with a cause.

Rachel was staring at Lana, thinking to herself how Lana was so much like Ray, which worried her. She wanted Lana to be more like herself and less like the wild and imaginative child she was already proving herself to be. At that moment, she decided she would come home slightly earlier than usual to bake a special dessert, a family favorite, in order to bond with Lana. There was only a couple of weeks before Lana would be starting school and Rachel wanted her to start off on the right foot.

It was a cold winter's night. Nana had made lasagna for dinner, and after they enjoyed that, Rachel started to make her favorite zesty lemon-poppyseed cake. She wasn't the best chef, but she did her best with Lana's assistance. There was a good amount of cake batter scattered in the kitchen, but Nana didn't dare disturb the special time they were having. Instead, she decided to retire to bed earlier than usual to leave them alone.

"Mama, did Nana teach you how to bake?"

"No, not really. Well, I was never really interested in cooking. The only reason I know this recipe is because your grandfather loved lemon cake."

"Oh, did Grandfather show you how to make it?" asked Lana.

"Yes, he showed me how to make it when I was about your age. I made it for him on his birthdays. I've made it a lot, that's why I can't seem to forget the recipe. And now it's become one of my favorites too," Rachel laughed.

"Well then, I think it will be my favorite too," said Lana.

Lana and Rachel smiled at each other and put the cake in the oven. When it was done, they enjoyed it with a cup of hot cocoa. The cake was sweet and tart and the cocoa was tasty as always. Cocoa was Lana's other favorite treat.

After eating and cleaning up after dessert, Rachel decided to light the fireplace in the living room, so they could be warm while they talked on the couch. Typically they were in bed by now, but Rachel wanted to prepare Lana for her upcoming schooling, and Lana listened intently. She loved being with her mother even if she was talking about the most boring of topics. They sat there for an hour or so discussing the importance of education and discipline, while the fire burned gently. Lana was then sent to bed while Rachel decided to stay up a little longer to work. She fell asleep sitting on the couch, working on paperwork.

A little while later, Rachel woke groggily to the heat and crackling of the fire blazing up to the ceiling, engulfing the picture frame above the mantle and daring to grow stronger still. She screamed over the flames, but no one roused. The walkway to the bedrooms was next to the fireplace so she couldn't get to the rooms from inside the house. She ran outside to Lana's bedroom first and pounded on the glass window, but Lana didn't move a muscle. The smoke had gotten to the rooms.

Rachel put her sweater around her hand and smashed the window, climbing through it like a ninja in the dark. A fearful mother's strength is unmatched, and she tossed Lana onto her shoulders like a rag doll and laid her in the yard far from the house.

Lana woke to see the flames escaping through the living-room window out into the moonlight, dancing in the most disturbing way that made her feel dizzy and sick to her stomach. The fire seemed to cry for her attention. It was a haunting sight. Lana was frightened until she saw her mother assisting Nana to the spot where she was sitting and knew they were all going to be okay. She figured her wings must have guided her safely out of the fire first and then saw Pachamama's shadows in the flames of the fire. Pachamama sang:

"Pause. Presence. Peace.

Thoughts of fear may come and go but pause and be still to find love and peace.

We get to choose loving thoughts over and over again. Every moment of every day is a chance to start again, and like the phoenix from the ashes, we can rise in love."

Lana felt peace and courage move through her. She looked down to see her necklace and then looked back behind her to see her wings resembled those of the angel she saw in the hallway that morning. Envisioning her wings fanning out to cover her family in her loving embrace, she felt assured she could keep Nana and her mother under her wings for protection.

"The child that feels responsible for the ones they love,
get to learn that no one is responsible for another.
It starts and ends within you.
Child, you will learn,
You are appreciated and loved for your courageousness,
but you must extend love to yourself first.
Love and receive love that is your purpose, release the
need to shelter others and simply be."

Pachamama ended her song, her message conveyed through emotions.

Lana felt like nature was benevolent and truly nurturing if loved and cared for in return. Her purpose felt like it was to embody her magic to show others how to be close with nature and shine wonderfully. Knowing that most beings were not like her, she wished her wings could extend far enough to be an example for all sentients.

Lana let the vision of her wings fade and fell asleep in her mother's arms.

When the fire department finally arrived, they were able to stop the fire from spreading through the whole house. The living room was destroyed, but everything else was spared.

It took weeks to get the place repaired and much longer to get the haunting memory of the night out of her mother and Nana's head, but this planted the seed for Lana's purpose, presence, and peace.

Chapter III

Peace by the Beach

As Lana grew older, her connection to her magic began to fade. Until then, she used her necklace as a reminder and used her sparkling imagination to feel close to divine love. In this way, she was able to stay powerfully close to her truth and was a wondrous beam of light to behold in a dim world.

One of her favorite places to shine was near the ocean. On warm Sundays, Rachel and Nana would take Lana to the beach for a couple of hours. By the sea, she could explore her magic and be left alone with her creations for hours while her mother was calmed by the waves and Nana sat peacefully, always encouraging Lana to play openly.

While Nana and Rachel prepared lunch, Lana swayed on the sand to the chime of the tides. If she listened carefully, nature always had a recognizable tune to dance with. The necklace lay on top of her heart space and suddenly blazed with a rainbow of colors that shot out in all directions, igniting her heart open.

When she was done dancing, she decided to play in the sand. She smiled, content as she created, and then put the finishing touches on her delighted sandcastle. The castle was home to a tiny royal crab living regally.

"Hello, Your Majesty. So how do you like my latest creation and your new castle? Isn't it grand?!" Lana addressed him in a noble attempt at an English accent.

"It's perfect Lana, thank you for the gorgeous land-scaping you did in the garden. It's fit for a king," said the king crab.

"You're quite welcome! Come this way here for tea time, the ocean view from here is the best." She pointed to the terrace where there was a table for two. "I must be going now; it's time to get back in the water, please enjoy King Crab!"

"Good day Lady Lana," replied the king crab.

Lana walked over to the ocean. She saw a familiar face sparkle at her in the water. Pachamama's spirit was in the sea, swimming peacefully. Lana always felt loved by nature, but she wasn't always sure who this reflection belonged to. Strolling into the waves that licked the shore, she looked up to see rainbow dolphins jumping and playing, and then suddenly a mermaid popped up out of a wave and swam towards Lana.

"Hi!" Lana squealed with excitement. She was always thrilled to see the princess of the sea with her striking pale-blue eyes, bright silver skin, and purple hair.

"How are you, sweet spirit? It's wonderful to see you again. Here's the treasure I promised to show you last time," said the ethereal mermaid as she handed Lana a beautiful shell. "It's a gift just for you."

Lana put it close to her heart and then held it up to the sky. The array of gold-and-pink hues shimmered in the sun, blinding her momentarily. She quickly looked back up at the gorgeous mermaid.

"This is amazing. I love it. Thank you so much!" She hadn't remembered them having met before but was too shocked to admit it. She remembered reading somewhere how rare mermaid appearances were and tried not to blink, as the mermaid might disappear under the water at any second. "You're quite welcome. It's very precious and should be treated with love and care. Just like you, sweet child. Will you remember that?"

"Yes. I will always," said Lana. She thought to herself, how could I ever forget?!

"Wonderful. Have a beautiful day today. I had to give you this, but now I must be going, I have an excursion to be headed to, with you know who," the mermaid motioned behind her, where a flounder was waiting. He waved his fin. "I will see you next time Lana. Say hi to King Crab for me, will you?"

"Okay, bye!" Lana yelled past the crashing surf.

"Bye Flounder!" She waved as she watched the mermaid disappear beneath the sea and then ran over to show Rachel and Nana the treasured gift.

"Look, Nana and Mama, this is a gift from my mermaid friend."

"That's lovely," Rachel said a bit too sarcastically. "Are you hungry, baby? Here, eat this." She held out a sandwich.

"That's beautiful sweetie. We will make sure to keep it safe when we get home, so you have it forever," Nana said sincerely, which warmed Lana's heart.

Lana smiled at her Nana, and then stared at Rachel. She shook her head no to the sandwich and said nothing. It wasn't a surprise that her mother didn't understand her, but it was still disappointing. Rachel never saw things the same way she did. It was as if she was covered in a veil of gray fog, so the vibrancy of life never fully penetrated her. Lana saw things with colors and clarity, and her Nana encouraged this way of seeing.

Lana was appreciative of her Nana but wished Rachel could see clearly too. She had no words for her mother, so she got up to display her light. This time she flowed and flittered with her wings. This was her way of encouraging her mother and those around to be and express themselves. Others might not comprehend it, but Lana was a mirror for others, reflecting who they truly were. Children of Magic.

Rachel didn't see it, Nana missed it, but Pacham-ama was glowing in the background, appreciative of the harmonious way in which Lana interacted with magic and nature. Her breeze gently caressed Lana's face and lifted the sand to glisten around Lana and the pretty shell. Lana felt tangible warmth and love. Her magic was still strong.

Chapter IV

Friends

Lana was turning six years old and had a single friend come to her birthday party over the weekend. A single human friend that is, from her first-grade class, but Lana also had friends from the forest and even from the sea join in on the festivities.

Nana baked the treats, (though not the lemon-poppy cake, which was Rachel's doing). It made the yard smell like a scrumptious bakery with the scent of desserts. There was a long table that seemed to extend out to the edge of the backyard that was covered in cakes, pies, biscuits with fresh jams, and sweet creams with berries. There were chocolates, caramels, cotton candy, and cookies too.

Rachel had gotten her a large crayon set with some blank booklets to draw in, but spent most of her time running in and out of the house, busy with weekend errands. Nana got Lana a beautiful china set for tea time. They drank hot chocolate and then later, bubbly bright-blue tea from the set.

Juniper, Marigold, and Felix were the first to arrive.

"We made matching party hats out of rose petals from the forest. Did you get a whiff of how sylvan they are? Let's all wear them and have a grand old time! You only turn six years old once, you know?" said Felix. In one swift movement he grabbed a chocolate cupcake off the table and ate it in one bite before even sitting down.

The fairies giggled with elation.

"They're stylish also! They combine perfectly with my necklace and birthday outfit. Thank you!" said Lana.

They all sat down, gave thanks, and enjoyed their cake.

"Your Nana is such a superb baker. Please do give my complements to the chef," said Felix.

"Yes, she's divine," said Marigold.

"Marvelous!" said Juniper.

Even the mermaid and the crab were there. Lana wasn't sure how they got there, but she was just happy to have them in the blow-up kiddie pool. They swam alongside the sycamore tree where Pachamama's presence was there to observe and take part in the festivities.

Lana's human friend Megan didn't actually join the celebration until it was close to the end, and by that time all of her magical friends had left. They had already enjoyed the entire morning together filled with treats, dancing, and play.

When Megan got there, Rachel surprised them both with freshly boxed pizza. They ended the celebration with a pizza party. Sufficiently full, Lana and Megan laid on their backs on the grass and watched the sky turn into cotton candy. They stuck their tongues out to taste and revealed which flavors they preferred. They stayed like that for a while as they watched the clouds form into all sorts of shapes. They saw bunnies, bears, hearts, and stars until the sky turned into dusk.

"How did you like your birthday?" asked Megan.

"It was all perfect. One of my favorite parts of the day was in the morning when the mermaid splashed water on Marigold and she fell into the pool and turned the water into a shade of glittery crimson. Marigold decided to swim for the rest of the morning and it was really beautiful to watch her swim around illuminating the pool with her fairy dust," said Lana.

Lana had mentioned the friends of the forest to Megan before, but they never seemed to come together at the same time.

"I don't know if you really are magical or if you're just playing with your imagination? Like we do when we pretend to bake or see the clouds make different patterns. I always seem to miss your friends," said Megan.

"Yes, well you'd have to be open and truly believe

in it to see it. If you aren't willing to sense the magic around you, then it's easy to miss," said Lana.

"Yes, well at my house we don't celebrate any holidays, and my parents told me that make-believe things aren't real. I don't really know if I believe, but I do like pretending with you. It's fun to play, and I like listening to your stories," said Megan.

If Lana hadn't been lying on her wings, she would have fanned them out with all her might to prove to Megan that magic did exist, but she thought she shouldn't push it. When the right time presented itself, she'd show the world. Instead Nana called them into the house as it was getting too dark outside and they raced inside. The day had been Lana's best birthday ever.

A week after her birthday, Lana was over at Megan's. Megan was sweet, and her parents let them play for hours outside in the mysterious backyard. They'd get to play without their imaginations being interrupted for hours.

Their house was on a large plot of land. It was a bit of a junkyard and had an extra house far in the back, a couple of motorhomes, and scrap metal on the far side of the yard, but it was filled with mystery and excitement for the girls.

They spent most of their time in the center where a couple of trees formed a small canopy that provided shade over their sanctuary. There was a patch of grass for them to sit on and the right amount of dirt to create mud pies and pretend to be eating delicate cakes with coffee as Lana told fairy tales that she created out of nowhere. Sometimes they'd play hide and seek around the junk, or dance in the sun and pretend to be gymnasts and do cartwheels until they got headaches. It was always great fun.

One day when it felt right for a story, Lana started.

"Once upon a time in a faraway land, there was a village with no color. In the center of the village there was a large single hill. At the top of the hill lay a saffron cactus flower amongst the colorless environment, patiently waiting to be discovered. Each day it blossomed with bright orange hues, but no one could see it to appreciate it. For many years it tried with all its effort to be found. One day a young child was born without sight and without hearing, but bore wings. When he was ready and old enough he flew up the hill and plucked the flower. The flower thanked the boy for feeling him and released fog from its petals that washed over the entire land with a peachy mist that once lifted, revealed a vibrancy of all colors."

Megan was fascinated. Lana went on.

"The villagers of the land wanted to know how the boy had known there was a curse and an entranced flower to reverse it. And why didn't the flower help him with his shortcomings? The boy glided up to the sky to convey an answer, as he could not communicate like they did. The villagers saw him but grew irritated as they didn't understand his way of imparting information and so they ignored him. They were still cursed as they didn't care to see things differently. If they had tried to understand him, they would have known that he was only special but in no need of being like them. He was perfect as he was...and if they had only looked long enough in the sky, they would have recognized that there are even more colors than the rainbow reveals. They need only gaze long enough to feel into it, stripping the old way of seeing. As the boy flew higher and went further away, he never did return to the world where no one understood him. Instead, he traveled elsewhere to a land of his own. Every year the villagers sing loud songs of gratitude to remember him by, and throw powdered colors into the flames of bonfires, so shades of the rainbow smoke billows to the boy in the sky. The end," said Lana.

"Wow, Lana. How do you come up with this stuff? It's so interesting and sometimes strange. But I like it!" said Megan.

"Sometimes I see it and sometimes I dream it," said Lana.

"What does it all mean? Why were the villagers still cursed?" asked Megan.

"The boy was magic. A guide, but the villagers weren't listening or truly looking. He couldn't stay there if no one was going to listen," said Lana.

"Wow. I get it. Sort of. I mean, I think I get it," said Megan.

"It's okay if you don't. Just try to let it sink into you," said Lana, with hope in her heart. They sat there silently thinking of the boy for a while.

"I have an idea. I'm going to call forth the fairy sisters if you'd like to play with us?" asked Lana. "They live very close to here, in the forest and I am sure you'd all get along wonderfully, if only you'd give them a chance?"

"That sounds fun!" said Megan, not really sure but willing to try for her friend.

"Okay sit there and close your eyes. No one is usually watching when I'm calling on them to come play, so just give me a moment to gather my will," said Lana.

"Okay," said her friend as she closed her eyes.

"Let's see." Lana placed her hands on her necklace and heart space, closed her eyes and imagined that she flew over to gather Marigold and Juniper on her back to bring them to where she and Megan were. In her mind's eye, she saw them in the willow in which they lived; they looked back at her with joy. Lana smiled and opened her eyes to see them there in front of her now.

"You've come! I'm so excited to introduce you to my friend Megan!" said Lana.

"Hello, child, it is so wonderful to meet a friend of Lana's," said Marigold and both fairies curtseyed in midair, sprinkling fairy dust as they moved.

"Hello lovelies. We want to also introduce you to a friend of ours. She lives here in the backyard. She's timid, yet has tried to get your attention from time to time, Megan. I think now is the perfect time to be formally introduced," said Juniper. "Butter! Come out so we can all see you."

"Oh, my goodness. You really do exist. I'm so sorry I ever doubted you Lana. This is amazing!" cried Megan.

A bright colored bumble bee came their way and spoke. "Hello there, sisters. Hello Lana and hello neighbor, I'm Butter the bumble bee," said Butter. As she flew closer to Megan, Megan could see how cute Butter's tiny expression was and how cuddly her fuzzy body seemed. This was her first time looking closely at a bee and she wondered why she was so afraid before.

"It's wonderful to finally make your acquaintance," said Butter.

"Pleased to make your acquaintance as well. I have seen you before but always ran away from you since my mother warned me about being stung. I'm sorry, that must have hurt your feelings," said Megan.

"Thank you for your apology. I was sad, but I understood why you might be frightened. Some bees get a bad rap, but we are mostly a friendly species," said Butter.

"Well I am so grateful to have a neighbor like you. I thought Lana was probably the only one to have special friends near her, but I feel an instant connection to you, and would love to be friends and play," said Megan.

Butter the bumble bee landed on Megan. Megan giggled at her fuzz and petted her. They all played together for hours until it got dark.

Lana was so pleased. She felt like her magic was spreading into the world around her and it felt so right.

They enjoyed a couple of summers in this way, until everything changed.

*

It was already the time when the color of the leaves signified change. The changing of the leaves inspired Lana to write a short poem and she brought it with her to show it to her friends in Megan's backyard.

"Winter rang with its chilly breeze,

Spring sang with its colorful leaves,

Summer came with its warm dreams,

And Autumn sprang out of golden leafy wings."

She thought she'd get up from that point, show everyone her own gleaming wings, and fly around the backyard.

She walked through the back gate to get to the backyard. When she arrived, she found mud pies and pretend coffees sitting out on the table, along with chocolate cupcakes and hot chocolate. This was unusual especially because Megan, Butter, Marigold, and Juniper all sat there solemnly waiting for her arrival. She instantly knew something was up.

"Hi, everyone. Don't get me wrong—I'm so happy to see all of you here and all of this lovely food, but please tell me what's wrong? I know something's up," said Lana.

"Well I hoped we could play first before I gave you the bad news, but it's impossible to pretend nothing is the matter," said Megan. The others bowed their heads and closed their eyes as they knew the news would hurt Lana.

"I'm moving this week, Lana. My father's got a job opportunity and he's making us all leave. I don't want to go but I have to. Mom and Dad said I can't stay with Butter because she's just a bee and I can't live in the backyard when a new family moves in! It just isn't fair! I'm so sad Lana. I will miss you forever."

"I will miss you too," Lana cried. She didn't get to share her poem that day. All that she felt was indescribable, and so she said no more. She let her friend feel all that she felt. Her heart ached terribly, and she held her friend while they cried and then enjoyed their last day together.

Lana was eight years old when Megan left. She had lost her best friend and never had a friend like that again.

The other children at school considered Lana to be different and a bit weird. She was ridiculed for never taking off her enchanted necklace. Only on a few occasions did some of the children at school talk to her and only once did she get invited to a party.

The weekend before Halloween, Sandy, one of the popular children at school, gathered with her friends in the courtyard to invite Lana in person. It was Sandy's Halloween party and the girls made sure to tell her it was a dress-up party.

"Hi Lana, why don't you ever take off that funny necklace of yours?" asked Sandy.

"Because it was a special gift and I cherish it dearly," said Lana.

The girls around Lana snickered and Sandy held back from jeering.

"Okay that's cool. Well I wanted to invite you to my dress-up party. We're all going to dress up as our favorite animals and I thought I'd be nice enough to invite you too since your friend Megan just moved. But I'm not sure if you could dress up if you won't ever take your necklace off?" said Sandy. The girls laughed. There was a moment of silence as they waited for a reaction from Lana.

"Well I'll see if I can make it. Thanks for letting me know." Lana said, trying to remain cool as a cucumber, though she felt nervous.

The day of the party, Lana decided she'd go and give Sandy and her friends a chance. She had chosen to dress up as a fox. She loved dressing up and equally loved foxes, so she really enjoyed preparing for the occasion. She hid her necklace underneath the costume, so no one could see it. Her cute little tail was sewn on to the back of a red-and-white jumper and she had sweet fluffy ears along with a bit of black nose painted on perfectly by Nana. She was having fun until she arrived at the party and realized that it wasn't a Halloween party at all, but a birthday party and she was the only one dressed up. Sandy and the girls around her waved and then laughed.

Lana had wanted to run and hide but instead pretended it didn't bother her in the slightest. She accepted that she was different, and this enhanced her connection to her imagination. She imagined that Felix the fox from the forest was there and the fairies too.

Lana didn't resist the fact that she was different. She couldn't remember who had told her, but someone somewhere once told her she was perfect as she was. She accepted herself, even loved herself. In doing so, she recognized that people weren't always to be trusted, but that she could rely on herself and her imagination. So, she had fun being like the mischievous little fox. She ran around the party, danced like no one was watching, cuddled with the large golden retriever, and enjoyed herself. No one interrupted her fun, just pretended she wasn't there, and that was fine by her. She left the party feeling pleased, yet exhausted. Being around silly humans could be tiring.

She never did bond with another friend like Megan as a child, and so she preferred to get lost in her imagination and her books. Feeling like an outsider was okay by her. She could always depend on herself, her magical friends, and her books.

Months went by and Lana recognized that books were easy, and she felt safe in them. Opening a book made her feel welcomed and comforted in the pages of fantastic stories of all sorts. Her imagination could be safely contained within books unlike in the real world of disillusionment.

Chapter V

The Fog of Disenchantment

Lana believed in magic far longer than the average child. With her powerful imagination, she resisted the disenchantment that comes with aging with worldly rules. On the outside, she excelled. She was perceived as different, yet pretty and smart. These outward qualities remained fixed to others, yet within, her true-self drifted astray, unable to resist the way of the world around her. She would soon enough lose her knowing. Eventually feeling how different she was, she began to feel lonely and isolated.

One day, when Lana was about ten years old, she was with her mother at the neighborhood grocery store. The market always made her feel uneasy with its harsh artificial lighting and hurried people. The shoppers seemed zombie-like and made Lana very uncomfortable. In addition to that, she had been so busy with her studies, house chores, and sometimes

lost in books, that it made her feel extremely detached
to not only herself, but to those around her.

Lana was in the only aisle she liked, the cereal aisle,
when she saw a new vibrant red-and-green cereal box
that reminded her of a shimmering memory. Then
she remembered how she used to love dancing with
fairies, and at that moment, she wished to see her
magical friends. With that desire in her heart, she took
a deep breath, placed a hand over her necklace, and
summoned them to come forth within her mind's eye.

Just for a moment, she imagined that the beautiful
glowing fairy sisters of the forest came to comfort her
and play with her in the aisles. Suddenly, Juniper and
Marigold flew out from behind the cereal boxes and
showed themselves eagerly. They glowed with this
heavenly aura, glimmering with soft purple, pink,
and golden hues that lit up the aisle with their fairy
dust. They invited her to rouse for dance and play
and detach from the cold store and its sleepy people.

Lana remembered she held the power to bring her
magic back with her imagination. She followed the
fairies in movement, while they flew and chirped happily, twirling and dancing together in loving reunion.
She felt phenomenal when she was able to release and
expend energy through movement, especially after
having been so stiff with her duties.

Lana giggled at the fairy dust that tickled her nose.
She took a deep breath with gratitude in her heart

and beamed with her own golden aura.

"I know it's been a very long time, and I've been very busy with homework and chores, but I've missed you! Thank you for being here." She was thankful and could barely believe this was happening.

"We've missed dancing and playing with you, Lana. We're always here whenever you need us," whispered Juniper. She flew up close to Lana and gave her a quick kiss on the cheek. Marigold blew a crimson-dusted kiss that landed on Lana's other cheek.

"I love to dance and play with the two of you, it's just sometimes I get awfully busy with my responsibilities, and I forget you're around," said Lana.

From around the corner of the aisle came Felix the fox. He jumped up, toppling Lana to the floor affectionately.

"It's wonderful to see you wearing your beautiful necklace Lana. You've grown tremendously since the last time we saw you."

"You look mischievous as always, Felix." Lana laughed and got up from the ground. "And Juniper and Marigold look stunning as ever. I've missed you all terribly."

Lana sadly remembered that she was told not to use her imagination and play with her magical friends when they were out in public. Her mother said to her that it was okay to use her imagination in private if it didn't interfere with her responsibilities, but added that it was getting close to inappropriate at this age and might disturb her development. Although she knew Rachel was trying to do her best, Lana felt misunderstood and always so lost when her mother discouraged her from being herself.

Besides Rachel's rebellious high-school moment with Ray and having Lana, she was always serious just like her father before her. Lana's mother wanted to be disciplined, and so she didn't like to play around. When Ray had left her, she became strictly determined to raise Lana and work while attending school at the same time. Being productive and staying busy was fine by her. She loved numbers and had graduated from college with a degree in finance. Accounting would be her love affair and a real "love life" could wait. It hadn't served her well before and then she had her daughter to care for. She never thought about her inner feelings as her attention was on a lot of things outside herself.

Rachel interrupted her daughter's fun and said, "What are you still doing over here? Stay close behind me. Please, I need you to handle the cart while I check off this list."

Lana sighed and sadly gestured for her friends to scatter and they vanished. She was extremely sorry, her heart contracting and aching, but she remained loyal to her mother and rushed over to grab the cart to follow. Just like that her imagination crumbled, her light dimmed, and her true essence faded.

Lana was helping Rachel put the groceries away in the trunk of the car when the wind picked up and blew leaves through the parking lot. Lana paused to look up at the leaves that lifted off into the sky, reminding her of her forgotten wings. She stood there trying to remember what they looked like, and was rushed into the back seat.

Pachamama was there in the wind. She danced with the leaves that flowed. When the wind shifted, it picked up colorful wildflowers, and a fanciful melody followed the dance up into the sky, and back down to flow with other beings in the parking lot.

"Grown-ups are always in a hurry. Keeping themselves busy so they never have to feel or think too deeply about why they feel so discontented being disconnected from me. If they paused and became grounded, they would hear me lovingly whisper in their ear."

Pachamama said this while simultaneously willing thunderous lightning to take form. "As you grow, you tend to lose your ability to hear me clearly, but I am always there. I never leave, not even when you're lost in your thoughts or actions."

The wind swept down, glittering with illumination around a baby carriage in the parking lot. The child giggled and cooed, smiling up at the sky. The first drizzle of rain hit his tiny toe. Slowly fog from the dew rolled in, and it poured rain.

Rachel thought aloud to herself, "My hair is going to get so frizzy with this crazy weather," and threw the rest of the groceries into the trunk of the car and slammed it shut.

Lana's mood mirrored the dark weather that swept over, depressed in the backseat of the car. She pressed her forehead to the window and closed her eyes. She was lost in thought when she missed Pachamama's faint whisper. Too tired to care, she looked up too slowly, and the rain poured down, covering her view.

Chapter VI

Soul Flew Away

It was during the week right before children were let out for winter break. Most kids were already making Christmas lists, but Lana hadn't started on hers. She had been busy with a school project and hadn't even read any of her favorite Christmas stories or sang any of her favorite Christmas carols yet. The house was filled with the scent of freshly baked cookies and the sound of Christmas music came from the kitchen radio.

Lana was working when the music and scent inspired her to give her imagination a chance with a toy story. Her favorite holiday fairytale stories had to do with visiting the crystal lake up on the way to the North Pole with its friendly diamond dolphins and rainbow unicorns. She loved creating holiday stories based around the North Pole and Santa Claus but hadn't done so since the year before, when she used to give her imagination a lot more exercise.

She picked up her dolls with enthusiasm for play,

only to realize that her imagination was too muddled to play with her magic.

"Okay guys, I know it's been a while but where were we?" Lana asked doubtfully. "You, Prancer, were saying something about the dazzling dolphins, am I right?" She squinted with impatience and didn't get a reply.

With a heavy heart, she sighed and put the toys down. Lana had finally forgotten how to create from her truth. As she put the toys away, her heart ached, but she thought to herself, *it's time to grow up.*

And for now this was true. Lana was growing up so fast, as she had many responsibilities given to her by her mother to keep her busy and out of "trouble." So Lana became an overachiever, not wanting to give her mother any worries. She got straight As in school. Rachel approved of Lana's discipline, but Nana was unsupportive of this strict behavior. On many occasions, she tried to get Lana to enhance her once strong creativity, but to no avail as the pull to get her mother's approval was incontestable.

Lana sat on her beanbag and put the TV on. There was someone on the news crying, and she changed the channel to a thoughtless show, going numb, as she let herself be swept away with a story that muted her senses. Her aura was dimmed and her necklace seemed faded. Nana knocked on the door and walked in slowly with a plate of cookies.

"Hi Lana, I was wondering if you'd like to draw with me while we munch on some chocolate-chip cookies. I'm trying out a new recipe for Santa, and I know you have a great crayon set you haven't used in a while? Maybe you'd like to start on your Christmas list tonight?" Nana asked tentatively.

"You can leave some cookies, but I can't draw right now Nana. I'm too tired. Besides Santa isn't real. That's what everyone at school says, and apart from that, I have a big test in my first-period class tomorrow." She paused and then sadly confessed, "And I know the tooth fairy isn't real because I left my tooth with a little piece of chocolate and a note I wrote very tiny next to the small lantern, and no fairy came to get it this last time. When I told Mom, she said she totally forgot about the tooth. So now I know that that was all you and Mom with Santa and the tooth fairy and the Easter bunny too. Really, I don't need a list, I just want to get a dress and a new pair of shoes, but I can tell Mom myself."

She was holding her breath as she rambled and gasped for air when she finished speaking. Hiding remorseful tears, she snapped her head back to face the TV and away from her Nana.

"Oh okay." Nana walked towards Lana with cookies in hand and sat next to her. "You're right, sweetie. Those things aren't exactly real—they're just fun for your imagination, but I hope you don't forget that there is still magic within and all around you. A different type of magic that is here and available to you anytime through your imagination." Nana said no more and kissed Lana on the forehead, sighed deeply and left the room.

Nana was such a sweet and kind soul. She always brought with her a warm presence without effort and lived lovingly and quietly. Constantly near her loved ones, she was ready and willing to please because it made her happy to see those around her happy. She could sense that Lana was transitioning like all children do as they grow, when the density of the world seeps in and weighs heavy on the heart. It was difficult to see Lana's sense of wonder and light fade, but Nana also trusted in the divinity of how all things happened and so she didn't spend much time dwelling on it. She was easy-going and loving with her beliefs. She spent her Sunday mornings at the church down the street and she prayed each day that things in her life and her family's life happened with ease and grace. This was her way in which she connected to greatness, to her magic, and walked lightly upon the earth.

Outside a rush of wind was raging to be heard. It was Pachamama as she bounced off the window and danced with gleaming colorful leaves that led up to the twilight sky. Lana didn't move or look away from the TV; she hadn't heard a thing.

Pachamama's golden aura radiated through the

window. Peacefully she sang:

*"What you must understand is that I will always
remain by your side, child, patiently waiting for you
to hear my whispers and to see your truth again. I am
forever near.*

I sing with the mesmeric melody that wills shivers.

I collide with the crashing waves.

I set with the vibrant sun.

I stir with the rustling leaves into the sky.

I am in all things.

*I knowingly wait for the moment you feel me, come
back to me, or become one with me again.*

I am naturally loving and enduring."

Pachamama's glistening outline remained by the window, but her winds and leaves swept over to the forest. The enchantment faded away, and the animals scurried off as the fog of worldly illusion covered the magic with a damp darkness.

Lana found growing up to be confusing and quite hard at times and met her experiences head-on with fierce determination. At this time, she was hardening only to be softened at a later time.

What she would find was that her experiences were exactly what were needed so she could learn how to transmute the love from within to throughout. Only with her precise knowledge and understanding could she transform her lessons into compassion and get back to her magic in right timing.*

It was on the weekend one morning, when Lana was about thirteen years old. She was in the backyard sitting on one of the lower branches of the sycamore tree reading stories from a book called Goosebumps when she got a big surprise. She still liked being outdoors but there was a distance with nature. Her connection was different than before, but Pachamama's essence was still there. She sang even while Lana read on.

"Life can sometimes be soft, and sometimes be hard. Life is filled with traumas large and small, full of heavy lows and some great highs. Without experience and lessons, there can be no understanding or compassion, sweet child."

Pachamama sang this compassionately as she supported Lana through the sycamore, trying to prepare her for what was to come.

Books kept Lana focused and pleased. Sometimes she'd read sweet, fanciful books but gradually they became darker with the passing of time and the swing of change. At that time, she was going through a phase in which she liked hearing about ghost stories and haunted houses. Spooky books thrilled her and shadowed her own pain and fear. Masking her own feelings by being consumed by the fright of someone else's story, she created less and became distracted by books instead. She'd be enamored for hours once she finished her house chores and homework of course, and Rachel didn't care what books she read as long as they were considered age-appropriate and only after homework was completed.

She was reading about a possessed puppet when her mother came over and gently tapped Lana on her foot.

"Lana, how would you feel if I told you your father was no longer missing and that he wants to speak to you?" Rachel asked tenderly.

"Ummm what? I would think you were joking, but I would think it would be amazing," she responded quickly, and felt a bit dizzy.

"Okay, sweetie. Well, I have a big surprise for you, and I'm not joking. Your father is in town. He found out where we live through your uncle and he's at your favorite café Friendly right this minute. I know that's a lot, but would you like to go see him right now?"

Lana shrieked, "Yes, of course!" Her face flushed warm, and her heart beat rapidly. She was unable to express the magnitude of what she felt with words or emotions, but her eyes widened, and her smile became unsteady. She was confused, excited, happy, sad and more. She had always wanted to say the strange words "Dad" out loud to her father, like other children got to. She had dreamt of having a father figure to discuss things with that she couldn't do with her mother. She had always felt something missing in her life without really recognizing it was him until now.

She imagined them talking about the stars and the galaxies in the universe. Visiting places like her favorite forest and tree, a distant memory from her childhood. The image of her sharing a cone of Oreo ice cream with chocolate syrup flashed in her mind, and she knew she'd never tell anyone she had fantasized about this many times before. She had butterflies in her tummy, and she felt a rush of warmth flow through her. She was nervous. She jumped from the tree and landed gracefully on her feet with the assist of her invisible wings. Beaming with excitement, she stepped forward ready to greet her stranger of a father with an open heart.

Mother and daughter walked into the cafe side by side. It smelled of coffee and burnt toast and was a bit too bright, making Lana feel hot and nervous. A friendly waitress walked them back to where her father was sitting. He was at the table with a purple birthday bag and a single balloon tied to it with a Coke in his hand. Her father smiled the same broad smile Lana had, and she noticed they had the same toothy grin. He stood up as they approached him, which seemed very formal to Lana.

"Hi, Lana, it's wonderful to see you. I can't believe how big you are. I'm so happy to finally meet you."

Without a moment's hesitation, she said, "Hi Dad. I'm so happy you're here." She hugged him tightly and wanted to cry but didn't.

He couldn't believe how open she was, how easily and readily she opened her heart. He was grateful but felt unworthy of this.

"I know I haven't been around, and it kills me that I haven't been here to see you grow. I'm really sorry it's taken me this long to get to you, and I hope you can forgive me. I know I missed a lot of birthdays, which is why I got you a little gift and a card."

He handed her the bag with a card that had a teddy bear on the cover. Inside it said, "Happy Birthday to my daughter." He signed it with "Love Always Your Father," and in the bag was a history book and a pink sweatshirt.

"Thank you, it's okay. I'm just glad you're here now."

She didn't really care for an explanation; she just wanted her dad, and now she had him right in front of her. It was like a miracle.

"I owe you an explanation. You see, I had gone on a trip from Central America to South America. I started in Guatemala, where I am originally from, and then just went further and further down south. The further I went, the harder it was for me to consider going back to the States. I was trying to find myself, but I was really just getting more and more lost in the jungle. I just wasn't ready to come back until a couple of weeks ago. The truth is, I got bitten by a snake in the Amazon and needed to come back to see a real doctor and get healthy again before traveling."

He paused and grabbed Lana's hands. "That's when I realized I needed to see you too. I'm sorry I've been so selfish. I've always thought about you and prayed for you. I hope you can forgive me and accept me for who I am. I'm not perfect, but I want to help you in any way I can."

Rachel had kept quiet the entire time but interrupted here. "She doesn't need your help. She's a straight-A student and doing very well actually. She just needs her parents like all children do."

He nodded. "I understand."

Lana talked about school and her accomplishments in her favorite classes. They talked about how they both liked to read books and laughed about how they had the same loud laugh and sense of humor. Lana was so much like her father, and she loved it. It made her feel proud to be like him. They talked on and on, as they both enjoyed chatting. It was getting dark and time for them to separate. He lived in the big city of Los Angeles, but he said he'd come to visit her soon and until then they could write to each other often. Lana's mother listened and was reluctantly happy that they met.

They parted ways, and he promised to stay in touch. Lana smiled and nodded, yet as soon as he left she felt this rush of insecurity and uncertainty flow through her. This was a strange and confusing way to feel about someone she admired and had longed for. It would be weeks filled with mixed emotions until she finally got a letter from him.

Dear Lana,

I hope you've been well. I'm sorry it's taken me so long to write to you. I wanted to say that I really enjoyed our time together the last time I saw you. I am so proud of you and how well you're doing. I wish I could also be someone you could be proud of. I wish I could tell you that I too did very well in school, but that isn't the truth. I had a tough childhood and had only been lucky enough to date your mother in high school for a brief time, but besides that, I haven't had an easy life.

Your mother didn't know this but, see, my mama was an immigrant from Guatemala and raised me as a single parent who fought to support us and find much work, so we've struggled a lot in this life. Your grandmother and grandfather passed away before you were born, but they were both from Guatemala. And although I loved books and learning, I had a hard time being a student and feeling different than the other kids.

I never graduated from school, and so I worked and still work part-time side jobs a lot, and that's why I like to go to South and Central America where it's cheap, and I feel accepted. It has been tough to feel comfortable when you don't feel safe and secure enough to find purpose. I guess I feel like I'm not good enough to be your father and that I feel like I might be a bother and a disturbance to you. I am very glad you aren't like me and that you are focused on school. I know you will always be safe within yourself. I understand that and yet I can't really grasp that in my own life.

I know this is a long letter, and I've rambled a bit, but I also know how smart you are and how you will understand. See, I still don't have my life together, but I am feeling healthy and ready for an adventure. I feel like I'm always looking for something and until I have it, I don't want to interrupt your life with my inadequacies and drama. I am flying out this weekend so don't write me back. I will write to you from somewhere in the jungles soon, but I just wanted you to know that I love you and am enormously proud of you.

Love Always,
Your Father

P.S. Say hello to your mother and Nana for me. They have done such a good job raising you. I am forever thankful for that.

Lana read this letter over and over again, hoping she'd see it differently and maybe find a treasure within it that would deliver her father back to her sooner. The hard truth was that that was it, and it made her feel abandoned by him again. She didn't understand why he had to come to visit her if he was just going to leave her again.

That would be the last time she'd receive a letter from him. Slowly she stopped thinking of him and her fantasy of having a father who understood her. She had been fine before him and would be fine without him again. This is what she told herself, and she let her heart harden, and a dark and thicker wall rose high to keep her safely secure within it, like most beings do after heartbreaks.

Lana had finally forgotten that she was pure LOVE, a magical creation made with pure intention. And until the truth returned to her, she would unwittingly cover up her confusion with numbing and thoughtless activities, unaware of the inner shifts that were taking place. The human experience wasn't an easy one.

The world had stomped on Lana's magic until it was beaten out of her completely, finally extinguishing her light. That night she lost her connection and it felt as if her soul had flown away.

When the moon was high above their tiny home, she felt this displeasure in her chest and a pestering need to take off her once beloved necklace. Trance-like, she slowly reached around for the clasp, took it off without looking at it, and placed it into a petrified jasper wooden box. She slipped it underneath her bed where she had other hidden treasures from her childhood, like the shell from the sea princess, and left them to gather dust.

Over the years, Lana gradually became more aware of the pain and the darkness that existed, and her walls grew higher still. Unknowingly consumed by fears and shadows, she distracted herself by putting all her efforts on achievements outside herself. The dark and light existed, and she had felt both at such a tender age.

In the right time she would learn how to revive the light within to illuminate the darkness, casting light on the shadowy walls in her mind and heavy heart. But until then...

Chapter VII

A Calling

After years had passed, Lana became accustomed to the dark and robbed of her magic, evolved into someone entirely different than who she really was. She was profoundly disconnected and determined to succeed in all things. She didn't know who she was anymore or what she really wanted, but she knew how to get lost in her work and focus on her goals. In this way, she became successful in her career, though she was unconscious, lost, indifferent to love, and blind to her true purpose. This has been many a person's definition of success in "advanced" societies.

Lana was twenty-one years old when she had accomplished all the things she thought would make herself and Rachel happy. She graduated from a great college, got a good job, a nice apartment in the city, had the perfect boyfriend in finance, and yet she wasn't truly happy. When alone, she sensed this deep nagging dissatisfaction in the pit of her stomach and began to recognize that something was wrong, feeling it creep up on her slowly.

She'd be sitting at a fancy dinner in the loud city with her friends or boyfriend gossiping or having empty conversations, when she'd feel the depths of how shallow her life was and how lonely she was, despite being surrounded by people she knew. Extravagance and frill could only partially mask the emptiness. In moments of grace, she could see past what was in front of her. A vision just out of grasp.

It was at her twenty-second birthday dinner after she blew out the candles and someone handed her a purple birthday bag with a single balloon, that something was stirred in her. A memory of her father and a missing part of herself was piqued, as if a gentle admonition prompted her to show up for herself. It hit her hard, and she suffocated in the realization that something was very wrong. Feeling lost, and unable to express what she felt, she knew she needed to make a change within herself. It started and ended in her.

This was the first step needed before she could act and although it was painful and difficult to acknowledge, she was lighter from recognizing and accepting the emotions she felt. Inner shifts were forming change.

That night she had an intensely realistic dream where she was walking through a meadow of golden sunflowers that covered the land as far as the eye could see. The flowers began to sing a sweet melody that gave her permission for her to transform into her childlike self. They sang:

"Dear little Lana you are who you are
You are a perfect little twinkling star
Always lovable
So perfectly adorable
You are love
Always and forever."

She hummed along and danced with the flowers that tickled her skin. A red phoenix flew near her and chirped in her ear. He guided her to follow him, and as she did, she recognized she also had wings of her own to fly with. These golden tipped wings looked familiar. They flew together low to the ground, grazing the tips of the flower petals and sipping in the fragrance of the sweet flower's essence. They were headed to the center of the field where a large single lotus flower lay waiting. It bloomed with a tap from her fingertips. In the center of the petals was the face of someone she knew. It was Pachamama and in her hands lay a single cream-colored seed for Lana. She reached for it, and as she did, the flowers in the field lifted to the sky and danced above her up into the cosmos and sang,

"We are loved, we are related in the light.
You are loved, you are the light.
Swing this way, let us remind you of your ways.
Sweet as the sun, Magic child, we are one."

She brought the lotus flower to her face to see it up

close, and for a moment she thought she recognized Pachamama. Then she woke. There was a car alarm going off downstairs, and she remembered the dream in its entirety. It felt so real. Several moments passed as she relished being in that dreamy state where magic still took place and then she drifted back into sleep without dreaming.The next morning, she didn't remember the details of her dream, but the feeling of expansion budded and gently softened her heart.

A couple of days later, on what seemed like an ordinary day, she decided she needed to get some movement in before going home from work. She went to her usual gym and was late to her usual pilates class, so she decided to try yoga. She hadn't tried it before, but had heard it was a good workout.

Lana sat on a provided mat when the radiant yoga teacher walked in. Like the sun shining to greet the day, the teacher introduced herself to the class as Sunny and explained that she was subbing today, so the class would be a little different from what they might be used to.

Sunny first guided them through a breathing session called pranayama and explained, "By bringing attention to the breath, we can bring attention to the present moment. Most people don't know how to breathe properly. They breathe very shallowly without nourishing. But by taking big belly breaths, we can help cleanse and heal the body."

They were then guided through a glowing meditation where for a fleeting moment, Lana imagined her inner-self glow. They did a restorative flow that was calming and meditative. Then they closed the class with a chant of Om. Afterwards, Sunny said something that resonated with Lana.

"The light within me honors the light within you."

This statement touched Lana. After the class, she waited till the last person left so she could speak with Sunny.

"I have to ask where are you from? And how can I learn to be more like you?" Lana laughed timidly.

"Well, thank you. Thank you for seeing me. First of all, I have to let you know that I am a reflection of who you really are." Sunny paused so Lana could sit with that for a moment, and continued slowly. "I'm from here actually, but I travel a lot. I like to visit a lot of high-energy places and conscious communities, where my spirit can flourish and integrate. Sometimes in the city it can be hard to be still and listen, but that is the grand challenge. I think you should come to my yoga retreat in Bali next month and see what I mean. It will help you strengthen your practice."

Lana partially understood and thanked Sunny for the invitation but politely refused, blaming her work for keeping her tied down. She was stunned and wasn't ready to comply with the intense YES that was inside her. She wasn't used to listening to her inner self, so she dismissed her feelings.

However, this experience, however seemingly small, had shaken her out of her slumber for a moment, long enough to make a shift deep within.

It brought up a memory of her childhood and she was reminded of a time when she was in her truth. It seemed so long ago, but she remembered this slight feeling of wonder, expansiveness, and lightness. Of wings. She was faintly glowing and then her phone rang. It was her boyfriend Sam asking her if she could bring some take-out from their favorite Chinese spot.

When Lana brought the take-out home, Sam greeted her with a kiss on the cheek, grabbed his food, and headed to the sofa where he liked to eat in front of the television. Lana wasn't very hungry. She was lost in her thoughts, dreaming of yoga and Bali. She hadn't taken a vacation since she started working with her company two years ago. Instead she liked cashing in on the vacation hours and seeing her bank account rise so her student loans could drop. She always thought she loved being super busy: never lazy, never still. But the thought of Sunny, who was literally brimming with iridescence, made her stop to dream about what a couple weeks of yoga in Bali would feel like.

And just like that, a small shift made ripples in her consciousness.

A week later she was still Googling all things Bali

and saw that flights were significantly cheaper. In a moment of beauty, she booked her trip on a whim. She felt thrilled and excited, yet also anxious and nervous. She had never traveled out of the States. This was going to be something big, and she could feel it.

Later that evening she broke the news to Sam. She was taking a vacation to Bali, and she was doing it alone. He questioned her reasons, but he didn't care much either way. Sam certainly had no interest in jungles or yoga and would rather take the cash than travel anywhere further than Miami.

Chapter VIII
Bali

Lana had flown in a few days before the retreat was due to start. The plan was to check out the area before she had a daily regimen. The retreat was located in Ubud, Bali, and it was unlike anything she'd imagined. There was lush greenery, the jungle, rice fields, conscious community, spirituality on every corner, and the best food she'd ever had. Lana wasn't a vegan, but since the vegan cafes were plentiful and incredible, she decided to give it a go and her body thanked her. She felt her morning lethargy lift, and her complexion brighten. She wandered all over Ubud, into the city and then into the jungle. She visited water temples and waterfalls and attended dance classes.

The day before the retreat she decided to see a healer even though she couldn't say why she was doing it. Gede, the healer, saw people out of her house. The homes in Bali almost always looked like elaborate temples with rich colors. Gede's home was no exception and in the front of the temple home stood a large statue of a Ganesh, the elephant-headed deity, who is the remover of obstacles and lord of success. Lana was taken aback by the statue and then she saw Gede in her ornate dress and warm smile. She gestured for Lana to sit in front of her.

"How can I help you child?" asked Gede.

"I've never been to a healer before, but I was walking by and saw your sign in the front. Also the couple that just left here looked refreshed and inspired. Is there anything you can tell me to help me with my life?" Lana asked.

"You will be fine. You have everything you need inside you. You get to listen to remember who you are. For now, feel into the comforts and liveliness of being. Glimpse what life is like outside the haze and let peace wash over you to see what life can be like, here in Bali," said Gede. "Now I must be going. I was supposed to be done for the day after the couple, but I felt you coming. It is my naptime now. Good luck."

Lana wasn't sure she fully understood what had been said but she felt uplifted after speaking with the healer. She walked away in a tranquil state, pondering the conversation.

The next day when the retreat began, it was relaxed but structured. There was meditation and yoga first thing in the morning, followed by a light and healthy breakfast. Then a ceremony in the afternoon, in which they come into a meditative, intentional, and reflective state. There was a healthy veggie lunch, stillness and integration. Then a cleansing and gathering, before closing with beautiful, nourishing dinners.

During the first afternoon ceremony, in which they all sat together in a circle for the mindful ritual, Sunny guided them to close their eyes, breathe into the present moment, and ground into the earth.

"Without alcohol, caffeine, TV, or any other numbing devices, you will notice that you start to feel more deeply. You will become more sensitive. In this way, you can allow the good vibrations to penetrate you deeply. Give yourself permission to feel into nature, the faith-driven locals, the strong conscious community. Peace and love are abundant here, and it is for us all," said Sunny.

Sunny also mentioned that it was a new moon, so they would be having a fire ceremony later that night and that it was a powerful time to set intentions. She continued, "We will each write in our journals all the things we wish to let go of, and once we're done writing it all out, we'll tear the page or pages out and burn it in the fire. In this way, we can relinquish the power of those old stories and rise up in love."

This was a powerful opening to the retreat and made Lana feel like she'd freed herself from some of the weight that she had been carrying on her shoulders. Making room for the wings she had forgotten. She felt lighter and expansive.

Every day was so extraordinary in its own way. Each filled with quiet and peace and so much love and openness. Lana had laughed, sang, and cried like she had never done before. The entire experience had her feeling fully awake for the first time since she was a child.

On the last day, she felt so sensitive and receptive. The day included a cacao ceremony, with cacao from Guatemala. This seemed like an interesting coincidence to Lana since she was half Guatemalan. Sunny decided to introduce them to plant medicine so they could be assisted in deeply feeling and opening more fully.

Sunny said, "With this cup of cacao, we set our intentions. I'd like to go around the circle and ask each of you to share aloud what your intentions are."

When it came time for Lana to speak her truth, she took a deep breath and spoke. "My intention is to stay lovingly open. I desire to create a life from that place in which I can spread love out into the world."

It was at the end of this gathering when Lana was lying on her back, in shavasana, when she heard a faint whisper, a thought that didn't take form in her thinking mind, bubble to the surface. "Guatemala."

Guatemala was where her father was from. She hadn't seen him or heard from him in years and had hardly even thought of him since receiving his last letter. She didn't fully understand why she should go

there, but she held onto it. It felt right. Like she was
waiting for those words to be heard. Finally, after
taking steps to climb out of the fog, she felt grounded
and like she could listen to this calling.

This trip to Bali was merely the first step in a much
bigger quest. Everything happens in right order and
divine timing. Sunny brought her to Bali and Bali
was taking her to Guatemala. For the right reasons,
because everything was happening for her, not to her,
she was receptive and ready to really listen.

The day she got back home, Lana fessed up to her
boyfriend immediately. Sam was sitting on the couch
watching some sort of sports game eating noodles
when she broke the news.

"Honestly, I've never felt fully at home here, and
never completely understood by you. Sometimes even
when I'm with you and our friends, I feel lonely and
lost." She paused to find the courage to continue. "And
that's not your fault, it's mine. I need to go off alone to
find myself and love myself before I can love another
person. I don't really even know what I'm looking for
exactly, but I know I have to go or I'll suffocate here."

Sam didn't understand. He thought everything was
perfectly fine and the trip to Bali was a strange fluke.
He couldn't understand what a calling even meant.

"I don't understand where this is all coming from.
Did you meet someone in Bali? Is that it?" asked Sam.

"No Sam. That's not at all what this is about. In

fact, this isn't really about you. It's about me. That might sound selfish but how can I give myself to you if I'm incomplete and don't even know what I want?" Lana knew this was harsh, but she had to be or else he might think they would still have a chance. "I'm doing this for me, and I just hope you can be okay with that."

"I just don't get you," stammered Sam.

"Neither do I, and that's exactly the point. I'm so sorry, I don't want to hurt you, but I have to go," said Lana.

Sam was upset with this revelation. He hated change, but knew there was no point in arguing with Lana for too long. She was stubborn and would have it her way in the end. So, after some huffing and puffing, he let her go.

This wasn't easy by any means, since she felt guilty for hurting him, but Lana packed her things before she could change her mind.

Ready to witness this transformation, Pachamama lovingly watched.

"In this reality, it is no wonder why so many forget how to believe in their magic. But suffering and pain are teachers, there to reveal to us our oneness by showing us how similar our ailments are and how we're all connected and the same. Fear not my beauty, for if you listen closely, you will hear my calling, I am always here to guide you back to you," Pachamama sang

harmoniously.

Lana packed and threw out all the things she wouldn't need any longer. What no longer served her was out! The wind blew inside the room, and the breeze touched her skin, giving her shuddering chills. She was on the right path, and although she was frightened of change, she felt it light her up on the inside, and the glow warmed her heart.

Pachamama continued,

"You have been shaken out of the fog, long enough to feel and listen. You are gifted with remembering. You will remember what your MAGIC felt like. What child-like wonder smelled like. What being connected to all looked like. Once more you will feel connected and come back into your magical knowing."

Lana left the apartment, never to look back at the man or the home she left behind. They were never for her for long, and with her only possessions inside a few suitcases and a backpack, she jumped into an Uber that headed for the airport. She took a deep breath, and a glimmer of fairy dust shimmered hopefully on her bags.

After heartaches and lessons, she was coming into awareness, ready for the journey to self-discovery. She felt this urgency and was ready to connect with the land in Guatemala, with her ancestors, and with HERSELF again. It was time to get away from the people and the places that made her feel lost and lonely so that she could hear more clearly and continue to listen to her heart. She was apprehensive, yet filled with enthusiasm.

The airport was alive and welcoming, and beautifully vibrant.

Lana walked through the terminal where colorful fairies gathered to light up her path.

Fully prepared for the journey ahead, she hopped on the plane with a one-way ticket to growth.

Chapter IX

Guatemala

Guatemala hit Lana with its warm humidity as soon as she departed the plane. She loved the heat, which soothed her like a warm blanket. She hopped into a friendly tuk-tuk, where the drive to the lake was enlightening and exhilarating. She saw the incredible view of nature all around her and felt at home and alive. She was in this beautiful foreign place where she felt comfortable and welcomed with loving kindness by the land and the people around her.

It was like Bali, but with a deeply rooted affinity.

She was taken to her AirBnb, where the tenant, a friendly hippie named Dan, was there to welcome her to the space.

"Hey," Dan said with a big bear hug, "you must be Lana. Welcome."

"Hi. Thank you," Lana said shyly.

"Your room is here." He pointed to a small bungalow, next to an open space where there were mats and a small table with crystals, stones, and singing bowls. "You're next to the altar and the kitchen over here is shared. The yoga shala is in that area down below, where the view is amazing."

"Awesome, it looks great," said Lana.

Dan gave her the 411 on the place and mentioned that many animals and pets roamed around freely, so she should keep an eye on where she stepped or sat. He introduced her to some of the furry friends that were still in the vicinity. Then they walked down to the shala, and Dan bellowed proudly, "And these human friends over here are awesome too. This is Alice and Sheila."

"Hi, I'm Lana."

"Hi. Welcome," said Sheila and Alice in unison. With genuine big smiles, they hugged her in turn.

"So where are you from?" asked Alice.

"I'm from LA."

"And how long will you be staying here?" asked Alice. "Umm, I don't know yet," said Lana. She had booked a one-way ticket intuitively without making plans.

"The best way to do it. Just go with the flow and see what feels right," said Sheila.

"Yeah, it's my first time here actually, I just kinda went with an instinct to come here. Don't really have a game plan. Just going with the flow," said Lana.

"You should always listen to your intuition," said Sheila. "You know what, you should join us for the cacao ceremony at sunset since you haven't any plans. It's such a beautiful experience with the view of the sun setting over the lake."

"That sounds amazing. What kind of cacao ceremony? I had cacao once in Bali during my retreat," said Lana.

The girls explained to Lana that this cacao ceremony was a beautiful gathering held for healing and heart opening. This one was a lot of fun because the place always had beautiful music, great cacao, and the view of the sunset was the best from that shala. They insisted she had to experience it for herself. Lana was super excited to go. She was surprised how quickly she was already being guided back to the plant medicine once again.

"You'll love it. We'll go down to the ceremony at five pm, k?" said Alice cheerfully.

The girls left to go to the lake for a swim and Lana decided to Google more on cacao. She found that cacao was the pure form from which chocolate came from, filled with antioxidants, vitamins, and minerals. It had anandamide, serotonin, theobromine, dopamine, and other components that made people feel good. It dated back to the Aztec and Mayan times. They used it for medicinal and ceremonial purposes and it was as common as coffee is now. She thought it was interesting that her ancestors had used this for so long, but she was only now learning about it.

Lana walked down to the center of town and wandered around the quaint traditional city. She bought some fruit to snack on, and then saw a poster that mentioned a meditation/yoga class that was beginning in ten minutes. She decided to join it last minute.

The yoga teacher warmly welcomed her to the class, pointing to where the session would be. There was a vast, inviting space with a mandala on the back wall and lush greenery that enclosed the surrounding area. There were mats, blankets, and bolsters stacked in the corner available for all the students.

The teacher sat in front of the class. They chanted, practiced yoga asanas, and at the end, they chanted again. That's where Lana felt herself glow again. It was faint but unwavering. After meditation, she felt grounded and had this feeling of inner peace wash over her. In a serene, meditative haze she meandered out of the class and back to her place, so she could prepare for the ceremony. She felt centered and entirely ready for it.

The three girls wandered onto a small natural path that seemed to zig-zag farther into the unknown. As they got close to the ceremony, Lana heard music that permeated her physical body and resonated with her soul. It called to her, and her spirit answered by dancing along. She followed the music and her roommates, who smiled warmly, and together they walked through the jungle path that led to the most epic space for a ceremony. When they arrived, they were greeted by a young shaman who welcomed them sincerely with kind eyes that smiled more brilliantly than a smile could. She had never met a shaman before but thought they'd be ancient and intimidating. On the contrary, he was young, very kind, and made her feel safe and at peace.

He guided them into the opening space where others gathered around in a large bamboo shala that overlooked a stunning view of the lake and the sun about to set over the volcanoes. Expansive and spectacular, it took Lana's breath away, and she felt a bit dizzy with the lightness that came over her. She witnessed a hawk gliding over the lake, and felt connected. She remembered the wings she used to imagine as a child.

"Oh my God," Lana managed. "This is incredible."

"I told you that you had to come. It's beautiful, and you haven't even tasted the cacao yet," said Alice.

Lana could have stayed there forever, staring into the sky but was pulled away to sit and close the circle that gathered on the floor. Someone handed her a cup of cacao.

"Welcome sisters, brothers," said the shaman. He took a deep breath and closed his eyes. "We bless this cacao, and we thank the cacao spirit for helping us to open our hearts. Come home to yourself. Allow this plant medicine to assist you with your truth."

The cacao smelled of earthy, dark chocolate. Lana savored the smell and the taste as she sipped the drink slowly. "It tastes so good."

It tasted chalky and bitter, yet sweet and spicy, making her think of a dark chocolate bar that had been ground up and mixed with spices.

She drank the cacao and it opened her heart, and lifted her spirit. She was tapped back in and remembered she was infinite possibilities, one with God, one with all. She felt this inner light glow intensely throughout her body.

"I feel tingly," Lana whispered to Alice with her eyes aglow.

"You're supposed to feel whatever feels right for you," said the shaman. "We use cacao for ceremonial, medicinal, and healing purposes. We harness this plant medicine gift to open and assist spirits in listening to their hearts and release that which no longer serves. You may find release through sweat, tears, or even giggles. Just feel deeply and let go of expectations. Whatever insights you may have were already there, just waiting to be heard by your open heart."

This is precisely what Lana had desired. It was an incredible revelation. She nodded and smiled at the shaman.

"In these modern days, most people are cut off from their capacity to feel. You've been taught to dim your light and turn away from your feelings," he said. "Now we release that old story; it no longer serves you. Allow the cacao to assist you in reconnecting with your heart and inner self, so you can feel deeply and live fully. Here in the present moment, we open your heart, so you can glow in your full radiance and remember who you truly are."

Lana glowed brighter still. Her aura flashed a bright pink and purple, and then her light stood still in a golden hue that expanded throughout the room and into the world around her. She was connected back to her true self. The beautiful tribal music got louder, and the room was luminous with radiant beings, shining and dancing with hearts open.

As Lana danced, something shifted and moved powerfully within her. She twirled a few times, and her inner child came out through her body to hold her hands, and dance with her. She cried with a smile as she gazed at her sweet innocent self. It was such a beautiful, powerful recognition. This was what she was looking for. This connection back to the truth of who she was, to remember she was love, light, and magic, and there was no doubting that again. It was an enchanting experience, and so beautiful to feel the love and connection, with people who thoroughly loved and accepted themselves and everyone.

After an hour of moving ecstatically, Lana needed to take a moment to sit down. She sat near the edge of the shala, took a deep, intentional breath, and gazed out onto the view of the landscape beneath her in gratitude. With so many intense feelings, she sighed, letting out tears that had been suppressed for far too long and recognized that through tears, she was releasing and cleansing something deep within her. Lana saw the black raven flying high above the shala.

"I have been sent by your ancestors to remind you of their love and support," said the raven.

A dense, hard wall felt as though it was crumbling away at that moment, making space in Lana's heart. When her tears ran dry, she felt lighter and more alive than ever. She smiled up at the blackbird and thanked her ancestors for their guidance. When Lana looked behind her, she found her child-like self there, waiting and watching with loving kindness. Next to the child was a pitch-black jaguar with golden eyes. In those eyes, she saw that the jaguar carried her father's reflection. He had traveled from the winds of the west and had been waiting a long time to finally see her again.

He said, "My dear child, I knew you would come. You are in the cycle of transformation, and I am here to show you that your ancestors and I are very proud of you. We are and always have been watching over you." He nuzzled her face and continued, "In my human form, I chose to leave because I was ill prepared to support myself and another in human form.

Years ago while in Guatemala, my vessel left the land, but my spirit remained to guide you and impart my love within you. I looked forward to this chance to tell you that I am always with you. Always. I am you. I love you."

Lana remembered the last time she had sat with her father in the café Friendly, and how his letter had crushed her. She recognized his spirit from his big brown eyes from their first encounter and felt deep gratitude for this love and support she had always hoped for. There was a deeply felt understanding. He wasn't equipped to be in her life in human form, but his spirit was still a part of her, guiding her.

They gazed lovingly at one another, and he nuzzled her one last time, filling her up with love. By seeing deep into his eyes and feeling him, she felt the divine love that is in all of us and was imprinted with it, taking his spirit inside her, their souls intertwined. The bond was sealed. Thus the jaguar's purpose was complete. He jumped down from the shala back into the jungle.

Just then, Pachamama's wind swooped through the space and danced around Lana, her inner child, and the essence of her ancestors.

This was a divine reunion. Pachamama sang,
"You come from divine MAGIC, child, you do remember now. And it is up to you to live from this truth and in your purpose, and then gift your magic to the world.

REMEMBER you have the power to awaken and rise into your truth at any moment."

Pachamama danced around the shala and sang to the beautiful beings:

"No longer can you deny my voice.

Now is the time to align and connect.

In the present moment, we can rejoice.

Reach out to me.

Open and feel my presence.

Because I have always been there watching you.

Loving you.

Waiting for you to awaken.

With your heart open, I rejoice because my whispers were finally loud enough to shake you from your slumber.

I rejoice as you come home to yourself more fully and I rejoice as you rise into your MAGIC."

Pachamama's spirit wrapped around the souls and her winds glided around the dancer's bodies.

The spirits in the room felt Pachamama's presence, and they danced past the sunset into the darkness. They didn't need the sunshine; their lights lit up with more incandescence than the sun could muster.

Lana felt her wings and remembered she was infinite possibilities. Her physical body may not be able to fly like the birds in the sky, but she could soar with her soul and feel the expansion in her light body. She was in her truth, in her power, and nothing could take away her wings.

When the girls finally tired out from the exhilaration of the ceremony, they walked back to their place. Lana went straight to her room. In the corner by the closet, where she got the best reception, she wanted to make a call. She called her Nana, feeling that her mother wouldn't understand, and neither would any of her old friends. She wanted to speak to someone on the outside who was sure to be understanding.

"Hi Nana! I just had to talk to someone outside of this world because it feels almost like a dream. I've just witnessed the most incredible experience ever, and I can't sleep after feeling like I've finally woken from sleepwalking?"

"Okay. Wow. What happened?" asked Nana, excited.

"I just went to a cacao ceremony!" said Lana.

"Oh, really cacao," said Nana.

"Yes, a cacao ceremony. A gathering where you drink cacao, aka chocolate. It helps to open your heart and with release and with opening up to your inner truths. It was so magical, and when my heart bloomed open, I saw my inner self first and then saw my father's spirit. I now know that he truly loved me then and still loves me now. It was as if he sacrificed himself in order to give me unconditional love in this way. As if in his human form he couldn't convey his love, or his purpose, and so his intention with leaving was gifting me with more love and power. As though he is continuing to live in my heart and live vicariously through me. Do you know what I mean? And wait Nana, you didn't sound surprised by the word cacao. Usually, no one even knows what that is." said Lana.

"I am so happy for this experience you've had, Lana. That is so incredible. You deserve to know that you are lovable and loved always. Your father loved you in his way and continues to love you." Nana paused to take a thoughtful inhale. "And no, I'm not surprised by the word cacao. I know what that is, and I am so glad you are experiencing it. I've never been to a ceremony, but I wish." Nana laughed with joy. It had been a long time since Lana had spoken with such excitement. She recognized Lana was brimming with childlike essence.

"Hmm. Yeah. It's honestly the kind of thing that can't be explained. It has to be felt firsthand. It's hard to put into words how powerful that experience was. It feels like I'm in love. But with life and with myself. Ya know? I don't know, I just wish you could be here. I wish everyone on this earth could experience this," Lana exclaimed.

"I wish too," said Nana, and coughed loudly into the phone, "but hey, I gotta run. I am very happy for you, Lana. Send me pictures and videos if you can. Maybe that'll give me an idea of what it's like. I love you."

"Okay. I love you too. Have a good night. Send my love to Mom," said Lana.

Lana put the phone down and realized that no explaining or videos could do the experience justice. This kind of occurrence had to be felt wholeheartedly.

That was it. Lana knew that the cacao aided people with tapping back into their connection with all. She realized right there that her gift was to be a reminder of how to connect to the divine. And she would do that by giving this kind of experience to others. Her MAGIC was to open others up to their MAGIC. With the aid of the cacao medicine, they could live more fully connected to Pachamama and their truth.

A big smile came across her face as her eyes widened. That's it! She wiggled and jumped on her bed and hugged her hands to her heart. It was like she'd fallen in love for the third time that night. She took a deep breath, closed her eyes, and prayed right there. She gave thanks to her ancestors, to Pachamama, and the Great Spirit for assisting her in this awakening. How grateful to love and feel loved so wholly and holy.

The experience was mystical and inexplicable, a feeling of euphoric connection. Lana knew she was wise, and an infinitely perfect piece of stardust. Accepting herself, embodying love and light, remembering she was MAGIC. She was a beautiful creation placed on earth to live in human form more closely entwined with all. To live out of love and see miracles through the eyes of a human vessel.

Lana was still drunk off cacao and love. She walked into the living room area where Sheila was sitting and gazing at the stars in the sky. The living room was an open space with no roof, so star gazing was a regular activity for the residents.

"I am still really awake and happy."

"I know what you mean. It's all those bliss molecules in the cacao," said Sheila.

"Guess so," laughed Lana.

"So tell me, what are you really doing here?" asked Sheila.

"I can't sleep."

"No. I mean here in Guatemala."

"Honestly, I felt a calling from the land. I know that my ancestors are from here. I believe they guided me here in order for me to reconnect with them, with Pachamama and myself," Lana said truthfully. "It feels effortless to open and connect here. Like divine timing, like everything up to this moment led me here to recognize my purpose. You know what I mean?"

"I love that. I remember when I first arrived, I knew deep down that I needed to be here. To connect with myself and with the land, mother earth, Pachamama. A knowing that this place would be healing for me. And it really has been. That's why I haven't left," Sheila confessed.

"I can see that. I feel like it could be really easy to

stay here in Paradise and never look back," said Lana.

"Exactly," said Sheila.

They mirrored the same smiling faces back at each other.

"Well, I'm off to bed. I think tonight warrants some space in my journal before I rest. Have a good night," said Lana, sighing happily as she got up to leave.

"Sleep well," said Sheila.

Lana walked to her room and wrote in her journal:

I love it here, and I can understand why so many peaceful souls want to stay here forever, but deep down I know that isn't for me. I know I must be courageous and share this magic with the people who are lost, that I must share my purpose with others.

I know I came for a reason. I feel like I have fallen back in love with me so that I can share from this generous spaciousness.

Maybe the point isn't to fall in love with someone and procreate. Perhaps that's a byproduct from the inner magic and this innate love of life.

But, maybe the point is to fall back in love with ourselves? For us to live in love.

All I know is that when I am fully prepared for the journey, I will share this experience with others! One day I will make a difference in this world by living in my truth and

bringing people back to the magic and that connection with Pachamama.

She knew that that would be a difficult task but a worthy undertaking. She fell asleep as soon as she turned the lights off and hit the pillow.

That night she dreamed she was dancing on the majestic lake and around it, the volcanoes were simultaneously erupting and spewing out warm cacao. The cacao shot up into the sky and dropped down in different forms: liquid, chocolate balls, and chocolate bars. Lana was covered in chocolate and elated. She tried to catch as much as she could in her arms, brought over what she could and sat down to feast on what the land had provided her.

The next morning, she woke with a sweet taste in her mouth.

Chapter X

Right Timing

A couple of months went by in a flash. Lana had gotten comfortable by the lake. She fit right in, working part-time at a small café by her favorite yoga shala. She made just enough money to get by. She didn't need much to live by the lake, and she was content as long as she could eat healthily, practice yoga, and attend cacao ceremonies throughout the week.

Lana's favorite pastime was walking through the town where she imagined cacao being prepared for ceremonies on every corner. There were shamans here and there in tribal attire. They brewed the cacao in preparation and the entire place smelled of earthy, deep chocolatey magic. The cacao from different Mayan family farms were all unique, yet all made for healing intentions, with their own distinct flavors.

Lana was aglow with excitement and adoration. Buzzing off the cacao, her senses were kicked into overdrive. She smelled the overpowering fragrance of the cacao, tasted and tested each brew. She danced from shop to shop, buying cacao cookies for later. The city was magical and took her back to a time where her ancestors and the entire town knew the power of this plant medicine.

"Lana, let's go to the lake, please. We've been waiting for you," said a slender black cat that sat next to a grey tabby.

"There you are. Let's do it," said Lana.

Lana's new best friends practically followed her everywhere she went. Her tiny sidekicks were the black cat, named Shakti (the Sanskrit word for the feminine power of the universe) and the grey cat called Citta (Sanskrit for the conscious mind). She loved their company, and they loved to spend time together at the dock by the lake. They'd take a nap next to her, and she loved being embraced by the rays of the sun with her toes in the water.

While the cats were asleep, Lana watched the lake transform into one made up of crystals, where dolphins made of diamonds liked to pass by from time to time to dance and dazzle her senses. The crystalline waters were beautiful to gaze at and the sun setting into its majesty was one of the sweetest pleasures. Time stood still when the sun kissed the mystic lake goodnight. She loved to watch the sky go from a rainbow of colors into darkness with only sparkling stars. When she tried to comprehend what that vastness was, this deeply felt awareness and expansion expanded from within. She loved staring in awe and feeling into it. The cats would get her attention in perfect timing for dinner. It was such an excellent way to play with her imagination and connect to the lake.

Lana knew she had a purpose and magic to gift to the world, but the world could wait. The lake loved her, and she loved it back. The cats needed her right now, and she adored their company. Paradise and the high vibrational energy that was felt there was hard to leave. In the meantime, she tried and tested all the different types of cacao, and took her time developing a plan for when she returned to the real world.

One day when the cats were probably hunting and couldn't be found, Lana decided to go to the lake alone and sit in reverent silence. She was meditating while watching the waters glisten in the sun when she felt a presence near her. It was a tall tan man with light hair, walking on the stones in the sand with his sneakers on. He looked a bit lost in thought but when he looked up and locked eyes with Lana, it was as if he had been found, as though they had both been seen for the first time by a counterpart. There was an instant deep connection, and they didn't even know each other's names.

"Oh hi. I'm sorry if I'm disturbing you, I didn't see you there," said the man.

"It's fine. The lake is for everyone, not just women meditating by the shore. I'm Lana, what's your name?"

The man introduced himself as Max. He was an artist and was visiting the lake for inspiration for his upcoming landscape series with a couple of artsy friends. He was the type of man who looked serious from afar until he spoke and instantly warmed your soul with the heart on his sleeve.

And just like that, Lana's heart had merely beat in a way in which to say, "Oh there you are." She was meant to be in that exact spot to meet this man, to be loved by him and love him. And so it was.

Lana and Max spent the rest of the day together, getting to know each other on a human level and intensely bonding on a deeper level. When they ran out of words, their souls danced above them as they celebrated their union. There was a knowing that was felt beneath words. This was what a divine union felt like.

Interestingly enough, they were both from the same big city and yet had to venture to this exact spot to find each other at this exact time. It was funny how that worked.

"So, back home, I work for my father's construction company part-time, but my passion and purpose is to create art. I paint oil on canvas, and honestly it's my own form of meditation. The art keeps me centered," said Max.

His presence was so calm and warm. He felt like home. Lana hadn't known a person could make you feel so comfortable, but he did. He spoke softly, slowly, and thoughtfully. Everything about his demeanor made Lana feel at peace. He exemplified a peaceful warrior. He was brilliant and determined, yet kind and humble.

"I brought my art folder up here to capture the sun setting over the lake, but I'd love to draw your portrait first. Would that be okay with you? You're shining so brightly," said Max.

"Okay. That would be amazing. I've never had anyone draw me before. Thank you," said Lana.

Max passionately sketched Lana as she sat there graciously. An hour or so passed and then Max sighed lightly and smiled.

"Okay I'm done. What do you think?" asked Max as he showed Lana his work. She looked at it delicately.

"It's beautiful. And so detailed. How did you do that? Seriously, it's brilliant," said Lana. It was magic.

"Thank you. It's easy when I have a muse beaming with beauty in front of me," said Max.

Lana gave him a hug and Max blushed from her loving embrace and the scent of her naturally sweet fragrance.

The two were inseparable from then on. When Max's friends left to visit other parts of the country, Max stayed with Lana. This was the beginning of their journey together. They hadn't talked much about the future, but he knew he'd follow her anywhere she wanted to go. He could work and create from anywhere in the world with his talent and capability. Until they needed to talk about plans, they lived in the moment and tenderly loved each other.

Chapter XI

Plans

Life was just magnificent at this time. Lana and Max spent so much time by the lake just being. In love and bliss, they lived in perfect harmony. They liked spending a lot of time at the spot in which they first met. They meditated together and created together. Lana, with her ideas and plans and dancing and singing, and him with his art. They were just themselves, and it was heaven on earth. It went like this for several weeks until this one day when Lana wanted to go over her plans for their future.

"I thought it would be nice to talk a little bit more about the future. I brought this business plan with me to read to you after lunch. I've been working on it for so long now and I know I've told you a little bit about it and it's perfectly written from my heart, but I just want to read it out loud for someone other than myself to hear. Maybe you can give me some honest feedback," Lana said and took a deep breath. "But first, I'm hungry. Should we go get vegan tacos for

Taco Tuesday or the raw pad thai? Hmmm."

"Tacos of course. And I can't wait to hear about your plan."

"Tacos sound incredible," said Lana.

Shakti and Citta followed the new couple and purred loudly in accord. They loved Max too.

When the vegan tacos arrived, Lana breathed in the fragrance of their sweet essence. They smelled fresh and zesty and alive. She savored every bite, taking her time to consciously chew and absorb the nutrients from the meal. Max was naturally a slow eater, which was an excellent reminder for Lana. The cats napped next to them.

The plan was entirely ready to be read after they were finished with lunch, but Lana got a call from her mother instead. It was urgent. Nana was in the hospital sick, and that's all Lana heard before becoming a bit disoriented, and she told her mother she'd be getting on the earliest flight possible.

Lana hung up the phone. Max felt her pain and held her hand. The cats looked at her longingly, shaken and sad. Tears formed, and Lana let them go. She didn't feel prepared for any of this, but now she had to go back. It was time.

Leaving the cats, her friends, and the lake, and flying back was done in a daze. The cats fully understood and gave her love as she departed. Back on the soil of her old life, she was overcome with emotions.

She was overwhelmed with feeling the low vibrations that emanated from the city and the people. Having Max by her side gave her some strength, and he was grateful to support her. They were on their way to the hospital when Lana asked their driver to stop at the city park first. She needed to ground into the earth, and she had spotted a large oak tree that beckoned to her.

Lana sat next to the tree, Max followed, and they became still and meditated together. She remembered her purpose wasn't to stay comfortable and quiet in the jungle, but to return to the chaos to share her magic with the world that needed it so badly.

She remembered that Pachamama was in the wind that embraced her body and the billowy tree that shadowed her. This was a reminder that she could be amid the chaos to show how the love and light could drive out the darkness. She wanted to prove that magic existed, by embodying light and connecting people to the truth. Even if it was hard, right now her purpose was to be the student and teacher of truth.

She overcame the fear and the shadows with LOVE and felt into her sovereignty. She was a dominant force of the light. She glowed. After half an hour had passed, they got up, and continued to the hospital. Lana went to her Nana's room alone.

"Nana I'm here."

"Ahh, mi ninita. How are you here? It's so good to

see you," said Nana with tears forming in her eyes.

"How are you? You scared me," said Lana, allowing the tears to roll down her cheeks.

"I missed you. I'm fine baby, I'm strong," said Nana.

"I know how strong you are Nana, but pneumonia is scary. It's also okay to be scared. I had to come here as soon as I could, and bring you love and strength. And see you, because I missed you and wanted to give you a hug too," said Lana.

"I missed you too. I was scared, but I honestly do feel better. I knew it was time for you to come back here though so I let your mom call you anyways," Nana proclaimed. "And knowing that you were coming back gave me strength and vitality. You literally light up the room with your energy."

They smiled and laughed. The tightness around their hearts loosened.

"I love you. Thank you," Lana said.

A peaceful feeling washed over them both. Everything would be fine. They embraced, and Lana had tears of joy because she knew she was ready to share her light with others too. "I'm so happy to see you and know that you're okay."

"Of course, I'm okay. I'm not done yet. And I love you too. Now can you tell me all about your trip and the cacao?" Nana said perceptively.

"It was incredible, Nana. It brought me back to myself. I feel like I've awakened from sleepwalking.

That's another reason why I'm here. It all has to do with the cacao," said Lana. "Also, I met someone, and he's sitting in the waiting room. But first, let me start from the beginning."

Lana carefully explained to her Nana her plans to use ceremonial cacao to create and share it with the world. Pachamama's wind danced and a couple of hummingbirds fluttered by the window. Lana grinned at the hummingbirds. They were there from the winds of the North, in the essence of healing, there to teach her to see the joy and magic even in rough places. Lana was ready to step into her purpose, and the winds flowed lovingly through the room. Lana felt a twinge of excitement run through her body after sharing with her Nana.

After a long hour in the stuffy waiting room, Max was welcomed to meet Nana. They instantly loved each other too. Max had that effect on everyone. It was such a beautiful gift to have. He gave Nana flowers, and they chatted and smiled and laughed. After getting to know each other, Rachel walked in, and things shifted in the air. She met Max and liked him too, but was reserved in showing him what she felt.

Chapter XII

Back Home

Lana and Max decided to stay at her mother's place. When they went into her childhood room, great big sobs rose to the surface. She felt everything so deeply, and it was a lot. She felt it without judgment, and released the puddle of emotions that were in her body. Then they lay in her tiny bed and Max held her as she cried herself to sleep in his arms.

Sometimes feelings come and go like this. That was the human experience. One minute one could be filled with courage and the next minute, tired and in need of crying it out. All of it was okay. Lana remembered Nana telling her feelings should always be felt and then looked at for clarity.

Hours passed, and Lana woke to find a big golden fluffy dog in her room. For a moment she had forgotten where she was.

"How did you get in here?" Lana asked, and the dog got close to greet her with a big slobbery lick. "Mom! When did you get a dog?"

"Oh, that's Bailey. He's a rescue," said Rachel.

"That's wonderful. But since when are you a dog person?"

"Since recently. He's good company."

"Oh wow. That's amazing. Wait, where's Max? Are you sure this isn't Max in another form?" laughed Lana as she cuddled the big fluffball of a dog. He was super cute.

Max was downstairs having a snack while Rachel fixed up a surprise dinner for them to enjoy.

"You're pretty cute, you know that?" Lana asked the dog.

"I sure am! You aren't so bad yourself," said Bailey and he licked her again.

"Oh, of course you can speak for yourself. It's nice to meet you," said Lana, grabbing his paw.

"You too. I've heard a lot about you. I'm glad you're here," said Bailey, panting heavily.

"Thanks Bailey. I'm glad you're here too."

They walked downstairs for dinner. Max was slowly snacking on some chips and guacamole at the kitchen table, and he motioned for Lana to sit next to him. Rachel had prepared a vegan casserole and a kale salad.

"Wow, this looks great," said Lana, inhaling the beautiful aroma.

"It's all vegan for you," Rachel said.

"Oh wow. Thank you for this, Mom," Lana said,

sincerely impressed.

"Yeah, I figured I could handle it for a little while. Max, are you also vegan?"

"I consider myself to be plant-based. I just try to eat consciously, and if my body needs fish, then I eat it mindfully and gratefully," said Max.

Lana put her hands around the plate and Max did the same. They closed their eyes as Lana blessed and gave thanks to the food for nourishing them. Rachel watched without mentioning or questioning it. They ate quietly for a while, and when they finished their meals, Max excused himself to freshen up, wanting to give them some time to speak alone.

It had been a long time since Lana had visited her mother. Before Lana had left for Guatemala, she hadn't visited in forever, always claiming to be too busy to visit even for holidays, and things were so different now. Lana was different.

"So, did you have a nice chat with Nana?" Rachel asked.

"I did. We spoke about a lot,' said Lana.

"That's good. Yeah, Nana was looking much better after she saw you. It was like the lights turned back on," Rachel laughed.

"I'm so happy she's feeling better," said Lana, amused at her mother's accurate description.

After dinner, they sat down on the couch with warm cups of tea in hand. Lana's mother wanted to show her a new show that was on TV. She loved having her daughter there and wanted to spend time with her, but she didn't know what to discuss. She always felt like her words got in the way, but she loved Lana dearly.

"You know what, I want to tell you something," said Lana. She wasn't interested in watching any TV. "I'm going to be staying here for a while. I have this plan I'm manifesting. I'm here sooner than expected but I'm going with the flow, trusting myself."

"Okay. I have no idea what you're talking about, but I will support you in whatever you want," said Rachel.

"Okay. Thank you. Well, that was easy. I wasn't expecting you to say that," admitted Lana. She went in with speaking her truth with no expectations. She thought she might receive some resistance at first, so this was a pleasant surprise.

"Why not?"

"Well honestly because growing up, I never really felt supported with my imagination or ideas. I honestly wasn't sure what to expect from you," said Lana.

"Baby. I was a single parent. I really thought I was doing the best I could, but I always felt like your imagination was too big, and I didn't want it to get in the way of you growing up, but times have changed." She paused for a moment to hold back her tears. "I have changed too. I always felt bad about the way I did things. I wish I could have done things differently.

I was young, scared, and a struggling single parent. I was hard on you, and I'm sorry I didn't give you the support you needed."

Rachel hadn't talked much to Lana while she was in Guatemala, but at the same time, she had been doing her own self-discovery. Nana had told Rachel about Lana's cacao experience, and it inspired Rachel to do some digging. It was as if it gave her permission to listen to her own calling.

She called it soul searching, figuring it was time for her to slow down with work and as she did, she changed too. She made time to attend church with Nana and found a hobby in ceramics and even dance. She started eating healthier and also got Bailey, although she was slightly allergic to his dander and would eventually gift him to Lana.

"It's okay Mom, I know you loved me and did the best you could. I realized you were only acting from a place of fear. I understand, and I love you." Lana paused to hug her mother and encouraged her to feel deeply into forgiving. "Everything happens in the right way. I learned that I truly only need that unconditional love and support from myself now and everything else is simply a bonus. I've already tapped back into my self-love and my magic."

"Baby, I appreciate you and love you to pieces. I always knew that you've had this magic inside you. I didn't know what it was exactly, but it scared me. It felt too powerful, sort of uncontrollable and unpredictable. But I can see that you harnessed your power, and I was simply projecting my fears onto you. I hope you know that I fully support you just as you are. I love you," said Rachel.

"I love you. Thank you," said Lana. She welcomed her mother's embrace. "Well, I'm happy to hear this because I'm going to open up a cacao shop and could really use some help."

"A what?" asked Rachel.

"A cacao shop. Where I'm going to have this beautiful space where people can open their hearts and come into their own magic," Lana said with excitement. "There is a lot I have to tell you."

Lana explained how she was going to change the world for the better with the aid of plant medicine. They would create a space where there was love and light and connection, where they prepared cacao with pure love and the intention to heal and open hearts. Where people would have a safe container to instantly transform into their childlike loving selves and tap into their truth. It would be perfectly cozy and inviting for awakening. Her mother listened intensely.

"It all sounds amazing, baby. I can imagine it completely," said Rachel with admiration.

"I'm really excited Mom! I made an appointment to meet with a banker tomorrow. I have a huge business plan, and I think it's perfect. I have it printed out here in my bag. Would you like to see it?" said Lana.

Rachel grabbed her reading glasses and took her time to read the plan carefully. When she finished, she slowly looked up. "Wow. I love it. The writing is beautiful, and I think it's very dreamy. But there aren't any numbers. For a business plan, you have to have a five-year plan laid out for cash flow and such," said Rachel.

"I don't know the numbers, but I think that when they envision the shop and understand the idea, they will support it. It's what I came here to do, it's my purpose." Lana said this with so much passion brimming in her eyes.

"I understand. I can definitely help you write up a plan, I just want you to understand that you will need numbers for the bankers," said Rachel with sympathy. "Hmm, but better yet. I can help you directly if we start small. I know the numbers for what a coffee shop looks like so I can work with that."

"Okay. Really? I mean, that sounds great! Honestly, it doesn't matter how small it starts because once the word gets out, it will grow into something grander than we can imagine. People will want this experience from all corners of the earth. People want to awaken and listen to their calling," said Lana.

"I have some money that I have been saving up for a while now. It isn't that much, but I also have my 401K. I think with that we should have plenty to rent something and start on it right away. And I have the perfect location," said Rachel.

Max joined them on the sofa but had missed the conversation. It didn't matter because he had been on the phone figuring out his own way to assist Lana with her dream. His father was a construction owner, and they would help Lana build anything she needed for her space. With love and trust, there we are infinite possibilities.

Chapter XIII

Pachamama's Principles

There was a tiny little studio space near Venice Beach that had loads of potential because of the location combined with their craftiness and creativity. This would be the haven in which all of Lana's dreams would materialize.

"This place is small and old, but it is prime real estate and a good deal. Luckily, I know the dude that owns it. He's a hippie and owns a lot of land, and fully supports the idea of having chocolate in his hood," said Rachel.

"Okay. Great, I can work with this. It's perfect for now!" said Lana.

"Exactly. We got this," said Max.

"Yiii Chicoyyy," Lana squeaked. This was the call of the cacao spirit. She twirled in a circle and hugged her mother and Max tightly.

Several weeks later, the cacao shop had a beautiful ambiance, covered in beautiful string lighting and greenery. Lana fit in as much greenery as she could manage without turning it into a jungle. The seating included beautiful vibrant cushions on the floor that surrounded small round coffee tables. The place smelled of cacao and freshly baked lemon cakes, and there were many fascinating books on the shelves to be read.

During the opening week it was a hit with some of the locals flowing in and out. A couple regulars were had within days. They had a man named Steve that came in daily for the lemon cake with either cacao or earl grey and he'd sit contently with a book for an hour or two. Shortly after that, there was an older woman named Davana that would come in with her tiny Chihuahua. She came in every other day for cacao, and couldn't stop raving about how it made her feel like she had her youth returned to her. Once the yoga community heard about it, things started to pick up quickly. They loved the message and supported it fully. You'd see them park their yoga mats in the front of the shop and gather before heading to yoga around town.

Two weeks after opening, Lana and Max started to hold cacao ceremonies for anyone who bought a cup of cacao on Fridays. It was a beautiful way to introduce setting intention with community and telling about Pachamama's principles.

"'Pachamama's Principles is an ode to carry in our

hearts: Pause, Presence, Peace produces Purposeful Paradigm shifts, & Positive Pandemics. I know it's a mouthful but it's easy to remember the seven P's."

The guests were smiling and beaming, intrigued. Lana continued.

"This means to pause and be still. Be fully present in the moment. Feel the peace within. This guides us to be the creators of a paradigm shift into a conscious and mindful community. Ultimately leading to a pandemic for more love, peace, joy, and MAGIC in the world."

"Let us close our eyes and with prayers in our hearts drink the cacao lovingly and intentionally," said Max.

This was a powerful notion and a parting gift for those that came and went. If you could get still, you could listen. Regardless if someone had had cacao or meditation or spirituality, they had been imparted with the knowledge that it was all within them to make a positive change in the world.

The word spread about Lana's magic, and the cacao shop became the talk of the town. When people entered the space, they could feel this palpable warm energy. If they were still enough, they could even notice that when they drank the cacao, a shift within them also occurred. Small shifts created ripples, and this is how it started.

After a few months of growing very popular, a kind

business partner came through to help Lana find a bigger space for the growth. It grew faster than they thought possible. The second location was as majestic as they imagined it would be. It was designed precisely how Lana envisioned it, like a welcoming tree house.

In the center of the space was a large willow tree like the one from the forest. There were other types of trees and plants that decorated the surroundings and more books on shelves. Conscious music, classical music, and Disney classics were always on shuffle and the scent of delicious baked goods such as croissants, cakes, pies and quiches along with the cacao drifted in the air. It was the perfect atmosphere for the childlike essence to thrive.

The cacao shop was a phenomenal place that was spacious and inviting for all kinds and especially for Lana's magical friends. The fairies could lay around comfortably in the oversized leaves of the trees, sip nectar from the flowers that sprouted, and watch the sweet spirits move around. The guests and the fairies equally loved it, and so did the stray cats and dogs. Lana couldn't get past the sweet and sassy cats to even notice what was happening above her head, but she felt the magic and the spirit of Pachamama. She was just too busy to really take the time to create with her imagination and was swept up in the magnitude of her new business.

The mention of an inspiring hot chocolate got

many curious people to visit the place, and the enrichment of their lives made them return for more.

Some gathered here for the connection and the love that was cultivated. They came and paused and took peace with them on their journey. Others gathered around for the weekly ceremony, and others ate cacao cookies or danced. Whatever expression took form was perfect. People learned how to fully open their hearts in this space. They also discovered the powerful ode that emerged from the magic. They carried this with them in their hearts long after they left.

Lana shared Pachamama's cacao medicine and spread love and light to other sentient beings. Because of her lessons, she could embody her truth. Lana used her magic for awakening, connection, and did her part in making the world a more MAGICAL place. This transformation was a gift to be recognized and to be deeply felt by her heart.

Max, Rachel, and Nana were all so helpful during this time. Max was usually painting but always joined in the Friday ceremony and stopped by almost daily. Nana and Rachel helped on the weekends. Even Bailey sometimes came with Rachel to impart loving energy. It was all perfect.

Chapter XIV

Cacao Shop

Lana spent most of her time at the shop with the large willow tree. She enjoyed the early morning before anyone else was there. It was her favorite place. She loved spending alone time there because she didn't feel alone, but connected to her ancestors and the earth. She spent a lot of time admiring the space and giving thanks for all the blessings in her life. She loved imagining her ancestors and feeling their spirits all around her, drinking cacao in her shop. She knew they were so proud of her for sharing this gift of plant medicine. She was her ancestors' biggest dream come true. She would be cleansing the space with Palo Santo and smiling sincerely, feeling the love that was all around and within her. This was her daily prayer.

Many times, she imagined her father as the jaguar and her grandmother from her father's side there holding space. It always made Lana so happy since she had never met this grandmother in person but felt a connection to her as well. Lana would blast her favorite music and dance around while she organized the shop and imagined her grandmother's spirit with the jaguar beside her to enjoy the dance.

One day she saw her grandmother fully in front of her, and Lana understood where she got her dance moves from, as well as her figure. She and Ray also had her grandmother's eyes and that same big smile. It kindled her heart to have these moments with family that couldn't be there physically, and Lana was so grateful for that.

Months passed and the message spread throughout the world, dispersing the magic far and wide. All around the country, the shops were popping up and becoming the place to pause and listen and tap back into the truth.

On the opening day of another one of Lana's cacao shops, she found herself in New York City. Rachel, Nana, Max, and even Bailey had joined her for this one. They always liked to travel with her to the different locations to assist her in cleansing and preparing the space.

"You get to be excited and nervous, it's completely normal," said Max. "We love you and are so happy for this new location. Are you feeling ready for the speech, my love?"

Lana was smudging the space. Rachel was dusting, and Nana was sweeping. Bailey was sniffing around and having a great time just being present.

"I am all those things and more. I'm so ready!" Lana laughed and embraced Max with a big hug and a sweet kiss smack dab on the lips.

"If you need me to help you with the speech, I'm right here. Ready and willing to help at any moment," joked Bailey and jumped up to give her a hug.

Lana came down to her knees, hugged Bailey close, and gave him a kiss on his cheek.

"I love you too. Thank you for holding such sweet space, Bailey. Thank you Max, for always being by my side. And thank you, Mom and Nana, for helping me with everything. You all mean so much to me and I couldn't have done any of this without you all."

"We love you and are so happy to help you, baby," said Nana.

"I second that. I love you so much," said Rachel and she came on to her knees to hug Lana and Bailey in a big bear hug.

They made such a beautiful team. Before they opened the doors to the shop, she gave a speech to the people that had gathered for the opening ceremony of this new location.

"Welcome all! Thank you for gathering here. This is such a special day. The word about the gift of the gods has taken flight all over the world. I couldn't be more excited about the healing that will take place here in this space and the beautiful vibrations that will emanate from here and the love that is felt will overflow into the world. The connection to yourself will be returned to you through your open hearts. I am so grateful for such blessings. I am so grateful for the fact that I can share the MAGIC with you all."

She paused for a moment and placed her hand on her heart. "And I also want to remind you that you can be still and listen and find the magic within without any cacao, and without anything outside yourself. We are all made of magic. We simply need to be still enough to feel it deeply. We must love and trust in ourselves and live from our soul truths. This is a practice. I am not above you in this; I am you. We are all going through the human experience and, we are all connected and must continue to rise in love and gratitude. This can be possible if we listen to our heart's call over and over again. Then we can embody our MAGIC on this life's journey and remind others how it's done. We can be the examples that others can follow to live life fully awakened. So, consider your-selves the reminders, showcasing infinite possibilities. We will make such ripples in the world, a paradigm shift that leads to a pandemic for peace, love, joy, and magic! Thank you for being here. Thank you for being. AHO!" She brought her hands to prayer and bowed in reverence.

"AHO!" The crowd cheered and applauded.

The wind picked up around Lana. Leaves rushed

up through the crowd and into the sky with dazzling flowers that flowed over to the park past a child and his mother.

Pachamama's wind willed shivers on the mother's arms as the two played in the park. The child stood still, feeling the crisp breeze and watched as a baby squirrel and a bluebird interacted affectionately. He glowed and giggled and then went back to playing with his mother. Pachamama danced in the wind and sang.

"Will you hear me whisper? Calling you, reminding you when you forget. Life is a great mysterious gift. And your purpose is to recognize it as such and create a life from that knowing. You are enough. When you forget, breathe and remember that love, peace, and joy are found from within. I will whisper always. Gently. But you must be still to listen.

Remember you are love and get to be a unique emanation of that love. You get to embody the light with your unique magic by just being you. When you embody your light, you glow from within, and others will see you shine, thus able to recognize their own radiance. You are enough because you are here now. You are perfect love. A Child of Magic. Be and let your magic illuminate you from the inside out."

Chapter XV

Change

Months passed, seasons changed, and Lana was changing too. She had her daily routines and rituals. She'd have her cup of cacao a couple of times a week and on the other days, a cup of pure herbal tea before she got to work on all things to do with the cacao shops. She attempted to keep her stillness amidst owning a growing business and the chaos of the world around her, but she was finding it harder and harder. Lana had quite a busy schedule that was taking her away from her ability to simply be. Her intentions of sharing her magic had become more significant than she could contain. She was only one person after all, and living in such a big way wasn't always easy, nor was it necessarily wanted. But things had proliferated beyond her control as they sometimes do.

Lana had been spending some time considering giving it all up. She'd been fantasizing about living in a cottage somewhere near a forest with her beloved partner. She never shared that information with anyone, but she noticed that she'd been thinking about it more and more and it was starting to feel more and more right.

One day during their weekend lunch date, Lana, Nana, and Rachel had decided to go to this cute little smoothie shop that was a block away from the cacao shop to get some healthy drinks that were quick and easy. Lana didn't like having long drawn-out lunches now that she was so busy. They grabbed their green smoothies and were about to head back to the shop when Nana gently grabbed Lana's arm and sat her down at the corner table, so they could all talk.

"What's going on, Lana? We can tell something's going on. Let's talk about it," said Rachel. Nana nodded in agreement.

"Well, you both know that I love what I've created, but I feel like I'm ready for change. It just doesn't always make sense. I thought my purpose was to share cacao with the world, but now I feel like my mission is fluid, like it's changing fast and I just can't make sense of it." She did know that change was constant, but she hadn't had the courage to discuss it until now.

"It's all perfect Lana. One moment you can share a large dream with the world and the next, you can influence a neighbor's life by merely dancing in the park and gifting him with the sight of your sparkle. It doesn't matter how vast your influence is, it just matters that you live from love and share your unique magic. That's the point," said Nana.

"Yes. Perhaps that dance sparked within him the inspiration to sing and for another to go write and another to be kind to a stranger. These little ripples affect the whole. And these types of ripples make waves of love that spark loving creation in others," said Rachel.

Pachamama's spirit was present as always and lightly said:

"Whatever your purpose is, whatever your unique magic is matters not. Your uniqueness is an expression of divine love. What matters is that you reveal it, and let it flow out of you to spread love tangibly for the world around you."

Lana sat quietly with this knowing, letting it integrate before she spoke or acted on anything. She knew what was coming.

With all of this understanding, Lana woke the next day feeling quite drained. She hadn't said anything that morning, but Max could sense something was off. He could always sense how his beloved was feeling.

He embraced Lana gingerly and spoke softly, "Lana my love, I can tell that something is off. What's going on? What are you thinking?"

He said this with such loving affection it melted a cold place in her heart.

Lana sighed heavily and said, "Truthfully I feel torn...I feel like I'm in the middle of carrying out my purpose with my cacao shops and now another part of me is feeling like I'm done with it, and I'm ready to slow down. The problem is people depend on me. They want more shops here and there. We have other countries that want the cacao experience, and I don't want to let anyone down."

He understood the pressure she was under and said, "Well that's intense. And this is going to be hard to hear, but I think the key is to recognize that you just said what we must do. We will slow it down. Honestly, I have been waiting to hear that for a little while now, because I was feeling that a change of scenery and pace was coming."

Lana smiled and nodded, "Oh really? And what were you thinking?" She was aglow, knowing that the conversation was perfect, and everything was happening in the right order.

"Well, I thought we should move somewhere where we can have peace and quiet at our front door. Where you can simply be, and I can paint. We can step away and enter the madness of the big city when we want to, but don't have to. Imagine a place near a lake or the forest. I know me and Bailey would love to get better air quality." He smiled and caressed Lana's hand.

What Max had suggested resonated so profoundly with Lana. She took the day to sit with it and later that evening when she felt ready to say the words out loud, she called her mother and Nana and expressed what she planned to do. They had been waiting for the call.

"I'm giving up my past purpose for my new-found purpose just like that. I'm listening to my inner guide. Just like you said Nana, I know it doesn't matter if I have a large audience or only Max, Bailey, and the two of you. My ripples of love make a difference in this world, and now my purpose is to be myself and live from love," said Lana.

"We're so happy that you know what you want and we're excited for you," said Rachel.

"We love you," said Nana.

Lana let her sweet business partner take over the company when he agreed to uphold "Pachamama's Principles" for her shops. He signed an agreement, and she walked away with her heart bursting open with approval. This is how she knew she was doing the right thing: when her heart budded wide open.

Chapter XVI

Magic Box

Lana and Max found a romantic, vintage cottage nestled in the town she grew up in, not far from Rachel and Nana. The backyard was spacious with a spiraling oak tree, directly next to a brook and the woods.

Inside the place was airy and intimate, with high ceilings, nooks, and alcoves perfect for cozying up and creating. It seemed seamlessly built for the two of them, and they loved it the moment they set eyes on it. It was an ideal place to create from a heart-opening space, perfect for Lana's imagination and for Max's masterpieces. Here, they could be easy and free. And Bailey highly approved of having so much room to venture around.

One day, a week after setting up and finishing with organizing and design responsibilities, Lana stumbled upon the petrified wooden box she had hidden under her childhood bed long ago. Her mother must have packed it in with the new things. She recognized it instantly and felt compelled to take a moment before she opened it. This was like uncovering a secret treasure buried deep in her heart. Butterflies filled her tummy and she took a deep breath before she lifted the top off the box.

When the wooden box was opened, the gift from the forest released aromas of sweet floral essence that triggered her memories of her childhood. There were dried-up flowers, a photo of her parents from high school, a rusted copper bee ring that she used to wear until she outgrew it in the fourth grade, some antique stamps, scratch-and-sniff Lisa Frank stickers, and the shell from the princess mermaid. So many precious items.

And then, Lana saw it, the glorious necklace from her darling friends. She looked at it carefully, and thoughtfully put it around her neck. It suddenly made her feel revitalized and alleviated. She felt Juniper, Marigold, and Felix's omnipresence and their adoration for her melted her heart. It was as if like a queen, she remembered to place the crown once more upon her head to be reminded of her God-given excellence.

Max was painting and Bailey was napping, so Lana decided to take the time for herself to wander back into nature's loving embrace.

She briskly walked outside her backyard towards the woods. She took her slippers off to feel the dewy grass under her toes. When she looked up, she saw a tiny red cardinal that reminded her of a phoenix and heard him sing. His song sounded familiar. She followed him with her eyes until he flew too quickly and all she could do was follow the direction from which his voice came.

Lana was still near the entrance into the forest when she saw this huge oak tree that reminded her of her childhood. She remembered she had had a favorite willow tree outside her neighborhood's playground and then the sycamore tree in her mother's backyard. She was undoubtedly fond of trees as a child, and this made her smile and glow tenderly inside. She was touching the knobby tree's bark when she remembered she could once conjure up her magic with her imagination. A voice rang out and sang in a familiar tone.

"Open your heart and be still,
Listen with a smile,
Magic child, the day has come,
To remember we are one.
Shine upon, sing this song, as the trees dance along,
The birds, the fox, and the fairies are your friends,
supporting you as you spread your wings,
Open your heart, open to what love brings,
Sweet as the sun, Magic child, we are one."

And then it happened. Slowly the tree's appearance transformed into Pachamama's spirit.

Lana gasped, and held her hands to her necklace

when Pachamama laughed with a majesty that echoed through the forest.

"Hello Pachamama, it's remarkable to see you again, to see all the beautiful creatures of the forest. I love you all," said Lana.

Some of the creatures of the forest were nearby and were heard rumbling around before emerging. The cardinal was back and kissed her on the cheek with a sweet peck, a white squirrel and her baby were at Lana's feet, and even a deer and its calf came out to nestle her. The forest's effervescence was dazzling.

Dark-green leaves opened to reveal their colorful flowers in bloom to dance in the breeze, the moss on the bark lit up with blues and purples, and the mushrooms and dead leaves radiated a golden glow on the forest floor. It was beautiful beyond measure.

She felt fairy dust touch her cheeks and she saw a group of fairies circle above her head before they delicately placed a large rainbow-colored rose behind her ear. She'd never seen a rose like that, and she giggled because she wasn't surprised to see the fairies. She had always had a deep connection to the fairies of the lands, and then it happened. It all came back to her, and she remembered everything. She had always had a deep connection to everything, to her truth, to the earth, and now to her magic again.

She recalled her visits to Pachamama and the forest from her childhood, the fairy sisters, the mermaids, the clouds, and the animals. She was in her magic, and she understood everything was perfectly timed. Because she listened to her heart and realized her purpose was perfect for her, she was able to be in her truth. She was a child of magic and gifted with the sight of truly seeing when ready to.

"Hello once again, child. This is the time in which you now fully understand that the power has always been within you."

Pachamama's essence from the oak tree fully emerged into form right before Lana's eyes and stood before her embracing her hands in her own.

"You are the love, the magic, and the gift...
I've waited for this moment in which we can celebrate
the lessons you've learned and this power you earned.
To rejoice hand in hand and dance with you once again.
To say I love you. I AM YOU.
I am so delighted you embody spirit through your light
and Magic by simply just being you," said Pachamama.

They hugged and merged into one. A beam of light shot out of the crown of her head and into the cosmos. Lana bowed to her heart in gratitude. She knew that they were always one.

Dozens of fairies danced around Lana's form. Their fairy dust scattered a rainbow of gold and silver brilliance all over Lana and the forest floor. Her wings appeared again and although her form stayed put, her soul took flight and danced in the sky. Lana had always been a Child of Magic, but she had to find stillness and listen to remember.

Hours later, Lana skipped back home singing the tune from the forest. She wasn't hungry after sipping on nectar and eating fresh berries provided by the fairies' brunch feast all afternoon, but she smelled freshly baked bread and knew that Max was cooking up a late lunch for the two of them and it would be tasty and savory.

She walked in through the kitchen door where Max was creating a delectable meal. He had prepared fresh green veggies and avocados ready to be spread on warm sourdough bread. He looked up to find Lana radiating a luminously golden hue.

"I love you!" said Lana melodically.

"I love you too, let's dance!" said Max.

He hummed a tune while they danced. This is how they knew they were in their purpose, when they glowed brightly so that their smiles matched their golden auras. All was perfect as it was. They danced hand in hand in the kitchen with so much love that Lana smiled and laughed with such magnificence and it was felt by all that dwelled in the forest. They expressed their uniqueness and breathed with magic, able to just live in love and simply BE.

Acknowledgement

First I would like to thank my beloved partner, Mike. I am so grateful for his love and support during this process. I'd also like to thank him for creating the book cover and the illustrations. Thank you to my family and friends that read the book first, and for all of those that helped me through the process.

I'd also like to give thanks to cacao. I wrote almost the entire book with a cup of hot cacao in hand. Please read more on cacao and see if it is good for you and your needs.

If you feel called, I'd highly recommend attending a cacao ceremony in your area, so you can experience it for yourself. Ceremonies are happening all over the world.

If you enjoyed this book, you might like a few recommendations on good reads and good stuff in general:

A Year of Miracles by Marianne Williamson

The Book of Awakening by Mark Nepo

The Healing Powers of Chocolate by Cal Orey

The Untethered Soul by Michael A. Singer

Oprah's "Super Soul Sundays" podcast

Yoga and meditation classes near you or on YouTube.

I am always learning and growing so this list expands all the time. I will keep you posted...

Love,
Christine Olivia

Christine Olivia Dargas has been writing since she was a child, expressing herself through poetry and short stories since the age of seven. Back in 2017 she lived in Germany with her beloved and wrote a short story about a little girl named Lana Livia. She set it down to move to LA and then in 2018, after nine months she finished the story A Child of Magic, based on her own transformational journey of remembering. Like Lana, she aims to cultivate love and enrich others with her truth and magic.

She lives in Los Angeles with her partner.

For more content go to www.achildofmagic.com